Stealing

Cyborg Seduction - Book Five

By Laurann Dohner

NORTH
LINCOLNSHIRE

Stealing Coal

by Laurann Dohner

Jill has learned the hard way that men can't be trusted and sex only causes pain. In the lawlessness of space, women are a sexual commodity—to be used and abused. She's doing a man's job, with only her father's brutal reputation and three androids to help keep her alive when she sees a massive, handsome cyborg chained to a freight table. The abusive crew plans to sell him to fight in gruesome death matches. It's stupid, it's insane, but Jill can't leave him to such a horrible fate.

Coal has survived being a captive breeding slave and irreversible damage to his cyborg implants, but his honor is still intact. He's grateful Jill saved him and he'll repay her the only way he can. He'll fix her—with his mouth, his hands and his body. He can teach the little human just how much pleasure she's capable of feeling.

Dedication:

Special thanks go to Mr. Laurann for encouraging me to follow my dreams and to Kele Moon, who became Coal's cheerleader as I wrote his story.

Cyborg Seduction Series

Stealing Coal

Editor: Kelli Collins

Cover Art: Dar Albert

eBook ISBN: 978-1-944526-72-6

Prologue

Explosions hurt Coal's ears and he realized he probably wouldn't escape the Earth shuttle before it blew up. His feet pounded down the hallway and he didn't dare slow, taking a blow to his shoulder when he slammed into the corridor wall. He bounced off and kept going as the lights flickered around him until he entered an open lift to take him one floor down.

The doors sealed and he clenched his teeth, hoping the power didn't fail completely. He'd be sealed in the small room, something he feared, trapped there to die. The lift dropped quickly and then jerked to a halt. Doors slid open and he realized he'd been holding his breath. He sucked in smoke-filled air and moved forward, fighting a cough.

Hope flared in Coal that he might make it out alive. Loud, angry voices drew him and he increased his pace, ignoring the burn in his lungs from breathing the contaminated air. He rounded a twist in the ship's belly and nearly ran straight into the small group of people clustered there.

Coal studied the two cyborgs locked together in an obvious tense moment. Ice had a council member pinned to a wall but he jerked his arm up to point at Coal. The weapon aimed at his chest lowered a second later.

"Coal? What are you doing on board? You should be back on the *Star*."

"With my damaged implants I couldn't connect to the shuttle computer." Humiliation hummed through Coal at having to admit his weaknesses. While he guessed the other cyborg males knew his flaws,

7

stating them aloud made the damage inside his head a little harder to take. He touched the scars on the back of his head, pushing away the memory of being strapped facedown to a hard surface and the pain he'd suffered while a female operated on him against his will. He'd been able to ignore the agony at first but once the implants were destroyed it had screamed throughout his body until he realized the terrible sound had not only reverberated in his mind but had actually passed his lips. He shook off the memory and continued, "I couldn't bypass the doors that locked me inside a storage room when I entered it in search of the remaining bots. It seems some doors you may enter but need a code to exit. What is going on?" Coal's gaze darted between the cyborgs and he wondered why they were obviously ready to engage in battle.

"No time to explain." Ice shot a glare at the council member, pure rage on his features, but then his expression softened when he turned his gaze on the attractive human woman.

Fascination transfixed Coal while he watched Ice and the female argue but he didn't see anger. He saw pain, fear, and heartbreak exchanged between them. It struck him immediately how strongly those two were attached to each other. He swayed a little on his feet when the gravity stabilizers on the shuttle weakened but then returned to normal.

His mind worked quickly, assessing the situation. Only two pods remained but four of them stood in the hallway. Ice wanted his woman to get inside a life pod to jettison to safety while the council member wanted to leave her behind.

Zorus wasn't a stranger to Coal. The male had fought hard to free Coal from the female cyborgs who had forced him to be a breeder for them,

8

using his seat on the cyborg council to assure that Coal got away from his abusers. Zorus had raged at the females over their treatment of a fellow cyborg in front of Coal, standing up for him. He'd even talked to Coal privately, offered friendship, and shared information—they had a common bond. Coal's abusers had been female cyborgs while Zorus had survived similar abuse at the hands of humans. Coal had appreciated the council member sharing his secrets to give him a sense that he wasn't alone in suffering the memories that haunted him.

Coal's full attention shifted to Ice. They didn't know each other well but he knew he could count him as a friend. His gaze lowered to the small female. The human stared at Ice with such raw emotions it stunned Coal. She really loved a cyborg. A human—one of those who'd attempted to kill the entire cyborg race—pleaded with Ice while openly admitting her feelings. The life pods were set up to support one life each. The gravity of the situation hit as Coal did the math. His eyes closed with the realization that two needed to die to give two a chance at survival.

He'd wanted to enjoy freedom, get to know his cyborg brothers, and become part of cyborg society. He'd been denied any sense of happiness by the females of his race when they'd crashed on the surface of a planet after escaping their own executions on Earth. His life had just begun anew when he'd found his cyborg brothers and for the first time in decades he'd been given the opportunity to embrace life with joy. His eyes opened in time to witness Ice knock Zorus out cold with a punch.

"Give him to me." Coal reached for Zorus, a decision made. Ice and his woman loved each other and they deserved a real shot at a future together. He and Zorus were emotionally damaged, probably not salvageable

9

anyway. Coal's body couldn't be repaired and Zorus had a bitter heart that rarely showed any emotion except rage, perhaps incapable of it after all he'd gone through. "You both need to escape now. I'll stay behind."

Ice didn't move. "Coal, you and Megan are taking the life capsules. I'm staying behind with Zorus."

It amazed Coal that anyone cared that much about him and only asked for Coal to protect his human from the council as a thank you for his sacrifice. Ice...trusted him. Amazement nearly floored Coal over the sheer magnitude of anyone willing to die so that he might survive. He felt honored.

Coal listened as the woman pleaded with Ice. She was willing to die with him before she'd leave him behind. Coal moved before he changed his mind. His fist slammed hard into Ice's face and he watched silently as the cyborg slumped to the floor with the already unconscious Zorus. He bent and grabbed Ice under his arms.

"Open a pod. I'll place him inside it and you take the remaining one. When he wakes, tell him to live a happy life for me, and that will make us even. I kept my promise. I protected your life since you won't be in any danger with a live male in your family unit."

The woman activated a pod.

Coal inhaled. "The fire has spread inside the walls, into the electrical conduits is my best estimation. It's just a matter of time before the damage is so severe that no life will be sustainable. We don't have much time. Open it."

The pod slid out fully from the wall and the woman activated the lid to open it. Coal adjusted his hold on Ice's large body, cradling him enough to lift him over the edge and settle him inside. The human only hesitated for a second before she climbed in after him.

"What are you doing?" Perhaps she didn't understand the specifics of the life pod. "These are designed for one individual."

"If he wakes before we're picked up, he's going to freak out and may get himself killed. If I'm on top of him, I can keep him calm and still." She paused. "And I'd rather risk both our lives than just leave you behind to die."

Coal released her. *Amazing. She'd rather die than be parted from the cyborg she loves.* A burning sensation in his chest caused pain as he watched her gaze at Ice beneath her. *Pure Love.* That emotion showed so clearly on her features that he knew he wasn't misreading it. Coal identified the source of his ache with one emotion of his own. *Envy.* No one would ever look upon him that way.

"You're brave."

"Actually, I'm scared shitless. I don't want to die, but if I do, I'm with Ice. It's the only way I want to go out. Is it just me or does this thing look similar to a deep coffin? Talk about irony, considering I might die in it."

Coal smiled. "I'm going to put myself and the council male into the last pod so we at least have a chance of survival as well. Good luck, Megan. You're worthy of Ice. He's a good male that I am honored to call friend. Tell him that please."

"I promise. Thank you."

11

When she jettisoned away he turned, staring down at the council member who had fought to give him freedom. They both deserved a chance to live and to possibly one day find happiness. As long as they breathed, they had hope. Ice had clocked the male hard, a lump already formed from the blow he'd received. Coal dragged the male out of the way, activated the life pod to open it, and gently dumped the unconscious Zorus inside.

He hesitated, not wishing to ever be locked up again but then the entire shuttle shuddered under his boots and around him. The acrid smell of burning wires threatened to choke him as it grew stronger. The shuttle emitted a high-pitched alarm, warning of imminent destruction. He climbed inside the tight space, lying chest to hip to thigh with Zorus, and activated it.

The lid sealed closed and the pod launched hard. The sick feeling in his gut assured him the pod shot away from the shuttle into space.

"Emergency life capsule activated," a female computer stated. "I am currently triangulating our location and will make exact calculations to set course to Earth. I will send distress signals for pickup of any Earth vessels we may come into contact with as soon as we are within transmission range of one. I am currently not showing any on radar."

Frustration roared through Coal. "I am ordering you to abort your protocol."

The life capsule computer hesitated with her response. "State authorization codes."

"Damn it," he roared, attempting to wake Zorus but he remained unconscious. Only Zorus could remote hack into the computer to change her programming. "You need to cut engines and turn this thing around now. You're taking me away from my people. You're going to get us killed. Do you understand? If you don't stop, we will die."

The computer didn't respond. Coal roared out in rage, his fingers curling into fists, unable to do anything as the life capsule headed straight toward Earth.

Chapter One

It's not my problem, Jill told herself, looking anywhere but at the center of the cargo bay. It became difficult not to repeatedly glance at the gray-skinned, mostly naked male, strapped down flat on his back and secured to a freight-loader table. *What are they going to do to him? Is he a cyborg?* She had no answers to the questions nagging her thoughts.

"My men just double-checked the manifest." The captain of the large C-class freight carrier smiled at her but his attention fixed on the front of her shirt. He didn't even try to hide his interest in her breasts. "Everything is accounted for. I'll transfer the payment if you just put your thumb here."

She moved closer and held her breath once she got a whiff of the man's obnoxious odor. He was another man who didn't care about personal hygiene, something she'd discovered often, unfortunately, in her line of work. She pressed her thumb down on the electric pad he held out and hid the wince as it jabbed her with a small needle to take a sample of her DNA to confirm her identity. She pulled her hand back, the machine beeped and she read the acknowledgment flashing on it as it completed the transfer.

"It's been good doing business with you, Captain Raul." She quickly stepped back, putting space between them.

"Now that the business part is over..." He flat out leered at her. "What would you say to some pleasure?" He winked, shoved the pad under his arm, and took a step closer. "I haven't seen a woman who looks as good as you do in at least a year. I could do all kinds of things to you. I hear redheaded women are fiery in bed."

She fought the urge to lose her breakfast and resisted the snort that attempted to rise. The guy had to be absolutely delusional if he thought she would be interested in having sex with him. She forced a smile when she met his gaze.

"Sorry. It's against the rules to fraternize with clients. Big Jim killed the last guy I hooked up with. You've heard what a mean bastard he is. He believes if I sleep with someone then he can't trust him anymore to do business with me."

Fear caused the man to take a quick step back. Jill relaxed. Her father had a widespread vicious reputation and was the only reason she hadn't been killed—yet. If they knew he'd died a year before and that she really ran his trading business now... She hid a shudder of fear, just considering the possibilities of what would happen. A lone woman dealing with the lowest forms of humanity wouldn't have lasted a week without being raped or sold into sexual slavery at a space whorehouse, and eventually killed. It could be brutal in space.

Her com beeped and she looked down. *Right on time,* she thought. She pushed the button. "I'm hurrying, Big Jim. Please don't get mad. They aren't screwing with me and the transfer just passed. Check it yourself. Please don't blow up their ship."

The captain of the freighter got a wild look as he backed up more, bumped into one of the boxes of food she'd just offloaded, and nearly tripped.

"Hurry up," a gruff male voice snarled. "I'm in a bad mood today and would love to kill shit. I'm monitoring every move you make. You need to undock my shuttle now to make the meeting point with my warship."

The com beeped, signaling the end of the connection. Jill peered up to see the effect on the man who'd just hit on her. He paled and his fingers gripped the electric pad so hard she wondered if he'd break it.

"He sounds mean."

"He is. Everything you've ever heard about him is all true." She pretended to be terrified. "I made him coffee he didn't deem hot enough last year and he broke my arm in two places. I once saw him skin a guy alive for cheating him out of a crate of gel fuel." The lies were easier to tell with a lot of practice. "He enjoys killing."

"You need to go now." The captain paled more. "It's good doing business with Big Jim. Please tell him we appreciate it a lot and hope to do it again soon."

"I will."

Male laughter had Jill turning her head to discover the source. There were four crew members surrounding the bound gray-skinned male on the freight table. One of them punched the helpless man in the stomach. The sound carried as fist hit flesh. She inwardly winced.

"Don't mind that."

Jill hesitated. "Is that a cyborg? I've never seen one before. I didn't even know there were any left alive."

"It was the damnedest thing." The captain's voice grew excited. "We were hailed by this life capsule. You know the law about having to respond

16

to all emergency beacons and intercept them. We scooped it up and there were two of them inside."

Glancing around, she frowned. "I don't see the other one."

"You won't. We contacted Earth when we found them to see if they were worth anything, hoping to score a big reward. I only told them I had one, you know, in case the government tried to pull any shit and they did." Anger tinged his voice. "They sent a battle cruiser right at us and forced me to hand it over to them. That one they didn't know about." He gave her a wink. "I'm real smart."

And heartless, mean, and a total jerk, she silently added. "What a brilliant plan."

"You know how Earth is." His lip curled. "Damn Government these days. I long for the old days before it all turned to shit when they began telling everybody how to live. The last straw for me happened when they started charging fees for surviving past a hundred and ten. It's a sad day when you literally can't afford to live there. They send out death squads to kill older folks if they can't pay up. They seized my cargo, spouting off some law I never heard of, claiming I had their property illegally. My ass. They just didn't want to pay for the cyborg. I would have fought it but they threatened to blow us up."

"That's why I don't live on Earth anymore." She tensed when she witnessed another crew member hit the restrained cyborg. He didn't make a sound but she knew it had to hurt. "Aren't you afraid they are going to kill him?"

"Naw. Those cyborg bastards are tough and my men are just warming him up. He needs to learn how to handle pain. I'm taking him to the Arris Station. They offered me really good money for him."

Oh shit, she thought. The Arris Station had become well-known and feared. If they were selling the cyborg there his lifespan would be pretty short unless he happened to be super tough. The station broadcast their twisted form of entertainment out to paying customers everywhere in the galaxies. They usually used criminals or mutated space pirates to put inside a locked cage together to fight until one died. The death matches were said to be so brutal most official programming signal senders wouldn't carry the option to buy the feed.

"Want to see him up close? I kept this one because he's got scars and looked meaner. The other one was kind of pretty and I figured he didn't fight much. I made a good deal with Arris Station. They really wanted him bad when I sent a vid of him. I not only get a flat-out payment but a small percentage of however many fights he survives."

Jill hesitated. Pity welled up inside her for the poor cyborg. Soon enough he'd find himself in a living hell far worse than the one he currently had been dealt. The captain took her silence for agreement and started to move toward the flat freight-loader table, leaving her to follow.

"Come on."

The crew torturing the poor gray-skinned male moved back, all giving Jill's body a thorough examination when she stopped about five feet from them. Her gaze wandered slowly over the biggest man she'd ever seen. They'd chained his arms above his head, stretching them high up, and muscles bulged in his thick biceps. His skin—a warm, sleek metallic gray—reminded her of the bulkhead color on her shuttle. She stared into his dark, furious gaze.

She forgot to breathe as they studied each other. He had really pretty eyes, though fury darkened them. They appeared nearly black under the bright, overhead cargo lights but she knew they weren't. They were probably deep brown. A low growl came from his parted, full lips, drawing her focus to them. There was no denying his handsome looks—in a rugged, strong-boned sort of way. The cyborg reeked of an overload of testosterone in her opinion.

"See why I kept him? Doesn't he look vicious?" The captain and his offensive stink inched closer to Jill. "Those are grade-four steel chains. He broke free twice from the lower density ones. He's a strong bastard and on his feet, he's six feet five—we measured him for the Arris. He weighs in at two hundred sixty pounds."

"That's big," she agreed automatically.

Her gaze lowered to his massive chest. She hid her horror at seeing darkened skin there that she identified as bruises. The crew had definitely been pounding their fists on the unfortunate cyborg. His stomach tensed, showing ridged muscles from his rib cage to the waist of the black, baggy shorts he wore. Her throat dried and she swallowed at the sight of how firm and in shape he appeared to be. She'd never seen anyone that muscular.

"We had to shoot him with five doses of knockout drugs to get him down. He's got a high tolerance to them so we're hoping it's the same for his pain threshold."

She nodded, unable to speak. His thighs were substantial, muscular limbs and his legs were bent at the edge of the flat surface, his ankles chained by more steel, securing them at the bottom of the freight carrier table. Her gaze jerked back to his face when he growled low again.

"Like what you see?" He had a harsh, deep voice that sounded damaged.

No one spoke that way, that roughly, unless something bad had happened to their larynx. They must have hit him there as well. Shivers ran down Jill's spine when she realized the cyborg was speaking to her.

He glared at the captain next. "I will break free and kill more of your men. You will all die when my friends come searching for me."

Holy shit, Jill thought. *Die?*

The captain took a menacing step forward and shook a first. "I lost four good men, you freak. You really want to taunt me?"

"I'm going to tear you apart with my bare hands," the cyborg calmly promised.

"Shut up," the captain snapped. "You want my men to get the shock sticks again?" He suddenly grinned at Jill. "Want to see something fun?" He turned his head and nodded at one of the men. "Get them. Light his ass up for her and show her how he jerks around. It's amusing as hell."

"No!"

She backed up and then realized her mistake as all heads swung in her direction, their frowning faces staring back at her. *Shit!* Her reactions needed to live up to being a heartless bitch who worked for the meanest, nastiest, bloodlusting trader ever born. Watching someone be tortured

20

should have been something entertaining to the character she played, not horrifying. She thought fast.

"I'm running late already and it's going to piss Big Jim off if I don't undock now. I never want to do that. You don't want to do that either."

The captain swallowed hard, his Adam's apple bobbing. "Yeah. You better get on your shuttle." He motioned to his men. "Let's store the new cargo. We can watch the freak suffer when we're done."

Jill had to look away from the struggling cyborg. He kept fighting the restraints in an attempt to break free, though it wasted his energy. She didn't blame him. He wasn't just going to be tortured by the crew but faced the eventual certainty of being beaten to death in a cage when he reached Arris. Pity and remorse slammed into her. Sometimes the shit she saw while trading made her wish she'd never left Earth. Not that Earth ranked that much higher but at least there humans attempted to hide their ugly sides. In space they flaunted their brutality as though it were a badge of honor.

Jill spun on her heel and forced her legs to move. Regret tugged at her conscience for the poor man she walked away from. *Is he a man?* She didn't know and her mind had no answer to give. She guessed he rated as one considering he must be made of flesh and blood if he could bleed. He obviously could feel pain. She had a limited education on the subject of cyborg history. Aunt Mary hadn't told her anything about them except the fact that they had been decommissioned for being too dangerous. Later, as she grew older, she'd realized what that entailed. The Government had slaughtered them.

Big Jim had insisted she be reared on Earth by his sister but Jill had been kept secluded from other people for her own safety. If any of her father's enemies—there were many of those—had known he had a daughter, they would have killed her long ago. The irony of using his name to survive as an adult hadn't been lost on her. As a child she'd been forbidden to even mention him for fear someone would discover her connection.

She lowered her chin when she approached her shuttle. "Open up, says me," she whispered into the com at the outer door.

The docking door slid upward and a ramp slowly lowered to the floor in front of her feet. She'd had to fly her shuttle up into docking port of the larger ship to secure it to the freighter. She glanced nervously around when she moved forward, her boots making a metallic sound on the thin metal floor, and breathed out a sigh of relief after she stepped inside the cargo hold. One more safe trade had been accomplished.

She turned then, peering out at the large cargo bay. Her gaze instantly homed in on the cyborg and she knew he would haunt her. Guilt could be a horrible thing. He still fought his chains, his muscles flexing and bulging, something she could see even from a distance. Her teeth dented her lower lip over the conflict his situation caused her.

"Close the doors," she ordered aloud. The ramp slid upward to return to the under floor she stood on and the shuttle door lowered to hide the sight of the cargo bay. She could no longer view the cyborg.

Jill stood here breathing slowly, her heart heavy from the reality that her life had turned to shit a year before when she'd received a message that her father wanted to see her. Aunt Mary had traveled with her and they'd met the dreaded Big Jim. His brutal lifestyle had finally taken its toll. He'd been on his deathbed and his body hadn't even grown cold before his crew of brutal killers revolted.

Hot tears burned behind her eyelids when she closed them. Aunt Mary had given her life to save Jill's. None of her father's crew had survived to spread the word that Big Jim had died. All she'd been left with was the shuttle she now lived on, her father's reputation, and the trading schedule on the onboard computer. She'd opened up an account with a space bank, used the cargo she'd found secured in the shuttle's hold to make her first trade, and her new life had begun.

The doors to the interior section of the shuttle opened and it pulled her from self pity. She turned at the loud noise to stare at Roid. His forest-green, artificial skin drew her attention first—not her favorite color but beggars couldn't be picky. She'd salvaged him from a dead ship she'd come across a year before.

"You are safe and we have another successful trade." His speech came out high pitched, almost feminine, but it had been the best she'd been able to do with her limited knowledge. "They paid?"

"Yes. I'm safe and the transaction went smoothly. We'll be set for a while."

The android stood there, unmoving, waiting for orders.

"Prepare for takeoff, please. You're better at navigating so you're in the hot seat this time. I don't want us to hit the sides of the freighter on our way out of the docking section. Wait for my order before we separate from them."

He turned, moved through the doors, and she knew he'd head for the pilot's seat. His programming included flying small shuttles, to her immense luck. She turned her head and stared at the closed exterior door toward the freight ship's cargo area. Though she couldn't see the cyborg, she still imagined him struggling against his chains in a frantic attempt to break free before they hurt him more.

The door opened behind her again and she turned to face it. Fray, one of the three androids aboard her shuttle, entered and stopped, his head tilted a tiny bit to the left, making him appear thoughtful. "Do you require assistance?"

"No. Strap in and recharge."

The android turned away to do as she'd ordered. Jill opened her mouth before she even thought about it. "Tell Arm to come to me."

"Of course," Fray confirmed, leaving the cargo area.

"Fuck," she muttered, shaking her head, and fought the disgust that rose in her. She walked to the cabinet by the door, jerked it open, and looked hard at the weapons stored inside. "What are you thinking, Jill?"

She sighed and after only hesitating for a few seconds, reached in to grab the gas-ball shooter. "Stupid, really insane, and pathetic," she muttered, hoping that hearing her voice aloud would make her reconsider her actions. Instead she spun around to glare at the exterior door. "Dumb, Jill. Really dumb. He's not your problem. You're a hardened trader, a bitch, just like your ex-husband said. Remember? Heartless shrew, cold-blooded hag. And don't forget frigid."

The doors opened and she winced when Arm entered the room. He squeaked badly as he came forward. She turned her head to watch him advance. He had extensive damage to his face and chest that she hadn't known how to repair. He looked hellish but there wasn't much she could do about it. The only thing on him not messed up in some way had been his left arm, hence the name she'd given him after she'd pulled him from a scrap pile on a distant junk moon when she'd discovered the android while searching for spare parts compatible with her shuttle.

"Orders, Sir?"

She'd given up on asking him to stop calling her that. He was military issue and had proven to her yet again that Earth Government wasted money by throwing great assets into the trash.

She took a few breaths and then blinked back tears that blinded her. "I'm a sucker," she announced to Arm. "You should call me that instead of Sir. Yeah, man down, Arm. He's male, gray-skinned, and the enemy has him in the cargo area just outside. What is it you always tell me about a man down when we talk about what happened to you?"

"We don't leave them behind the way they did me." Arm turned his big frame toward the weapons cabinet, and studied the contents. "How hostile is the threat?"

"They aren't military but they are hardened criminals. No kills, okay? Chase them out of the cargo bay since we need to blow the seal. I don't want them dying when the air vents out."

"Understood. Advanced scare tactics, grab our man, and retreat."

"Exactly." Jill wanted to smack herself over her hasty, stupid decision. The cyborg wasn't her problem but that didn't change her mind. "Um, he's injured so do not free him from the restraints. He's on a flatbed freight table so bring him inside on it. Repeat that order. It's important. Do not unchain him."

"I don't understand. He's our man." Arm spun to stare at her with his strange glowing eyes. They didn't match since she hadn't been able to find two lenses the same color but they were better than leaving him without cover for his sight sensors.

"He's been tortured and I'm afraid he'll hurt me," she admitted softly. "He needs to learn that we're not the enemy before I can trust him not to attack. Is that clear enough?"

"Protecting Sir is my number one priority. Order is understood." Arm spun around, grabbed weapons from the locker, and then faced her again. "You provide cover while I retrieve our man down. That plan puts you in the least danger."

"Got it." She moved to the wall and hit the com. "Roid?"

"Yes, Jill?"

"We're undocking hot once we retrieve some additional cargo." She paused, pushing back the fear that gripped her. "You may have to blast through their docking sleeves to shake us loose. Monitor Arm and me. As soon as we're back inside the cargo hold with the freight, get us clear. Don't wait for me to order you to start engines. They have cannon flares so heads up and try to avoid allowing them to hit us if they open fire."

"Understood. I will get us free from this ship and full blast with evasive maneuvers. I haven't failed to do that yet."

Yeah, we've been in this situation a few times before, she remembered with a flinch. She took a deep breath, released the com, and then ground her teeth together. She ripped a breathing mask from the wall near the door and tossed it to Arm then grabbed another and tugged it over her face. Her gaze locked on Arm while she gripped the gas-ball shooter with trembling hands. "Let's do it. Make sure you put that mask on him so he doesn't choke. You are in charge of this mission. I'm a green soldier."

"I have taken remote control of the doors." He moved forward. "I will take incoming fire until you're able to lay down gas cover safely. I will retrieve our man. Stay behind me to shield yourself, Sir."

She moved behind the big defense model android and said a silent prayer that this wasn't going to be suicide. It was crazy, stupid, and flat out insane to steal a cyborg from a ship the size of the freighter. She didn't want to think about losing an opportunity to make more money from dealings with this ship in the future, but she figured if she just left, knowing what the fate of that poor bastard would be, she could never face herself in a mirror. Even Jillian Maris still had moral lines she wouldn't cross.

"Go," she whispered. "Before I chicken out or remember I don't have a set of balls."

The exterior doors opened and the ramp slammed down hard when Arm hit the fast release. The loud noise made Jill's ears ring. *Damn Arm and his military tactics,* she thought. He'd wanted to make an entrance and he certainly had. She opened fire, the gas balls whistling through the air and exploding into the deck across the large cargo bay as she turned the gun to spread them out. The smoke rose instantly, spread fast, and shouted alarm came from the surprised men who found themselves in the midst of the unexpected attack.

Arm set off down the ramp and took careful aim to spread out more gas pellets near his perceived enemy without hitting them. Jill's gaze darted around, happy to see only four crew members in the cargo bay, all of whom rushed toward the exit doors to escape the smoke that quickly filled the room. The retreating men hopefully mistook the harmless yellow, smelly smoke as poisonous when it temporarily blinded, disorientated, and choked them.

Arm moved forward quickly, tearing across the cargo bay toward his target. Jill glanced at the cyborg, his expression openly shocked while he watched the android rush toward him to shove the breathing mask over his face. Arm grabbed hold of both sides of the freight table and then sped back toward the ramp, dragging the cyborg and freight carrier into the cargo hold of Jill's shuttle.

Jill jumped out of the way and backed up as the door across the large bay opened. The captain who had flirted with her rushed forward with a gun in hand. Their gazes locked before the smoke doubled him over in a fit of coughs. Jill fired again, laying down more gas balls between the captain and her shuttle to prevent him from shooting at her.

"We're in. Go!"

Jill dropped her weapon, tore off her mask, and grabbed for the wall to find a handhold. The sound of the ramp retracting and the doors slamming closed assured her that Roid heard her. Something pinged on the exterior of the shuttle and she flinched, hoping nothing would breach the outer hull. They would have no choice but to leave the freighter, leaking air or not.

The engines roared to life, making the floor vibrate hard. Jill flinched at the thought of the damage that could be done to the old shuttle by forcing such a cold start but knew there were no other options. She heard when Roid opened fire on the docking sleeves to force them to release the sealed grip they kept between shuttle and freighter. The room lurched, nearly sending Jill to the floor as they moved, a loud metallic groan reverberating throughout the cargo hold. She turned her head to stare at Arm, gripping the mute cyborg who remained motionless while he gaped in obvious astonishment at Arm's face just a few feet above his. The android carefully lifted the mask off him.

"Dig in and hold him," Jill yelled.

Two popping noises assured her that Arm followed her order. Jill winced again. Floor panels were difficult to fix but then the shuttle shot forward fast and the engines powered to maximum. Pain tore up both Jill's arms as she clung to the wall to avoid being thrown around. Arm didn't move and he kept hold of the cyborg. Jill's weapon wasn't so lucky. Metal scraped the deck before it slammed into a far wall. Once again she wished for better gravity stabilizers.

"We are clear, evasive maneuvers, and full burn." Roid's girlish voice could barely be heard over the racket the engines made. "I'm not reading any hull breaches."

29

As soon as the vibrations were manageable Jill released the wall and turned to face her guest. He'd recovered from the astonishment of Arm, his attention now fixed on Jill when she moved forward.

"Hi. I'm Jill." She paused, not sure what exactly to say to the cyborg since she hadn't planned to steal him in the first place. "In three days we're going to reach Hixton Station in the Gambit system. When we get there I'll set you free and give you enough money to shuttle you wherever you want to go."

The cyborg had really beautiful but frightening dark eyes. He gave her a chilly stare but said nothing though his full lips pressed tightly together. He took a deep breath but didn't speak as seconds ticked by.

"Okay, I guess you don't want to share your name. That's all right. You're aboard my shuttle. I'm a trader, and against my better judgment I couldn't leave you behind after I heard what they were planning to do to you."

He still didn't respond but instead watched her until it made her nervous. She knew he could speak and that he understood English since she'd heard him make threats. The silence grew uncomfortable. Jill backed away a few steps since she could practically feel the angry vibes coming off the big gray guy. She shifted her gaze to Arm.

"I'm going to send Roid in here to babysit our guest. Do not release him."

"Understood."

"I thought you stated I'd be freed." The cyborg's raspy voice startled her.

Jill met his cold gaze. "I said I'd free you when we reached Hixton Station."

He fought the chains, his body tensing when he strained, but the restraints held. Pure rage narrowed his glare.

"I'm not breeding with you."

She took another step back, reeling from his staggering announcement, and skimmed her gaze over his gray skin. His words sank in and unless he spoke a different version of English, which she highly doubted, his words implied sex. She openly gawked at his powerfully built chest and ran her gaze down his long, massive body. She shivered with fear at the mere concept. He was the biggest male she'd ever seen, besides her bulky androids.

"No worries there. I'm not suicidal and you aren't my type. I didn't steal you for sex."

"That's why females keep males tied down and restrained. If you aren't going to force breed me then release me now."

"I don't know you and I enjoy having the ability to keep breathing. You're going to stay restrained until I know that you won't hurt me." She paused. "That will be when I have Arm push you onto Hixton and release you after you're off my shuttle."

He literally growled at her. It was a deep, scary sound that reminded her of a vicious dog she'd once found trapped in a ditch. She'd rescued it and the thing had promptly bitten her once she pulled it to higher ground. She subconsciously rubbed the scar on her upper arm. *No good deed goes unpunished.* She could still remember her Aunt's voice telling her that as she'd tended Jill's wound twenty years earlier.

Jill backed up, putting more distance between them. "Okay then. You stay here and growl. I'm going to go pilot the shuttle but one of my androids will make sure you're fed if you're hungry. I'm well stocked so you'll have plenty to eat as my guest." Her gaze flicked over his body once more. He didn't look as if they'd starved him. She turned away. "Just tell one of them you're hungry when you want to eat."

"What is *it*?"

She froze, and then frowned over her shoulder. The cyborg stared up at Arm, studying him with a perplexed expression. Arm watched him too. She took a deep breath.

"He's a military android I found and salvaged. Earth Government had tossed him into a trash heap on a dump planet. His name is Arm and he's not an 'it'. I have two more of them, Roid and Fray. Please don't call them anything but their names. I'm very fond of my guys. They won't hurt you but they won't take orders from you either. Their first priority is protecting me. They are loyal and it's a rare trait these days that I appreciate."

The cyborg frowned at her. "I'm going to break free and take control of your ship. I may show you mercy for saving me by not killing you."

"Great," Jill muttered, storming toward the door. "It's official now. I really am a sucker. I'm going to have it tattooed on my ass in big block letters

Chapter Two

"He's requesting to be freed from the chains." Roid hesitated. "Arm stated he's our man. We should release him. He isn't acting irrational."

Jill wished she'd learn to think before she did things. If she did, she wouldn't end up in these messes. "He's dangerous so no, you can't free him. He's to remain locked down. Did you feed him?"

"Yes, Jill." Roid watched her. His two-colored eyes were sparking, making her feel guilty for not being able to fix him properly. She had to look away not to flinch when his left eye flickered on and off rapidly.

"Just tend to him and make sure he has what he needs." She checked the screen again to make sure the freighter wasn't coming after them. She knew when they'd blown their docking door seals that it would slow the freighter down, hopefully damage the bigger ship enough to keep them from coming after her at all, while they made repairs. She wanted to put a lot of space between them before they recovered. "I'm going to stay here and keep monitoring our scans to make sure that freighter isn't in range."

"It would be irrational of them to hunt us."

"They are people, not computers, and logic doesn't mean a thing to them. Humans are emotional and they really seemed to want to keep the guy in the cargo hold. Some people get pretty testy when you steal something they highly value." She hoped Roid understood.

"May I move him into your quarters?"

"Why?" The question surprised her. "I told you to keep the cargo hold warm so he'd be comfortable. I remember he's not fully dressed." The memory of the mostly naked cyborg flashed in her mind. All those muscles he had were fascinating. She pushed that image aside, knowing how wrong it was. "If he's cold, adjust the heat again."

"You have a bed. Real people sleep on those."

Jill turned her head, bit her lip, and looked directly into Roid's sensors. "I don't know how to explain it to you but that wouldn't be a good idea."

"Is he not a real person?"

Shit and hell, she thought. Sometimes trying to teach androids things had to be the most difficult thing she faced in her day-to-day life. The androids tried hard to learn everything they could and she even considered them friends. She knew they weren't actual living beings, but they had the ability to adjust as they picked up new facts to save in their programming, and they were all she had. She tried to go with logic since she couldn't exactly tell Roid that there was no way she could sleep feet away from a chained male who wanted nothing better than to break free. As for having him sleep in her bed? She pushed that thought away fast, not even willing to go there.

"He's real but he needs to be where he is. Real people don't share a bed or quarters unless they are a couple, which we're not. He's going to have to make do until we reach Hixton Station. While I'm thinking about it, could you please go through storage and see if you can locate some of those discarded men's clothing we have onboard and see if something might fit our guest? That way he's got an outfit to wear when we drop him off."

34

The idea of leaving the cyborg in nothing but the skimpy, loose shorts he wore had her imagining what he'd look like standing up. *Probably pretty terrifying*, she thought. She sighed. She really didn't need the trouble stealing him had created but leaving him behind would have bothered her more. She looked up from the screen to find the android still watching her.

"What?"

"Are you ill?"

"No. Why do you ask?"

"You've been less talkative since we left the freighter."

"I've had you babysitting our guest. It's not that I don't want to chat with you but I'm avoiding the cargo hold."

"Why?"

Yeah, why? Her mind paused on that silent question.

"You have a real person on board to talk to but you haven't gone to see him. I don't understand. Logic states that you would spend as much time as possible with him. You are always lonely, Jill. We're aware that we lack certain qualities other people who are real would give you."

"You're real to me." She reached out and touched his hard-shelled body, rubbing what passed for his skin, feeling cool rubbery substance under her fingertips on his arm. "Did he ever tell you his name? It's hard to speak to someone when they won't talk back."

"He refuses."

Her hand dropped. "I'm fine. I'm just a bit worried about that freighter coming after us. Our guest is probably worth a lot of money to them and they aren't going to just let him go without trying to recover their loss."

Roid turned away to leave the piloting section of the shuttle. "He is requesting you."

"Well, shit," Jill muttered as she stood. She wondered what kind of threats the cyborg would make this time. She dreaded every step of the way. If it were up to her, she'd avoid him the entire trip to Hixton.

Warm air hit her as the doors whished open and she hoped she hadn't set it too high for his comfort. Then again, she didn't want her mostly naked guest to be chilled. What she saw when she stared at him made her jaw drop open.

"Shit!" Her astonished gaze drifted over his chest, his lower chin, and his throat. "What happened?"

A dark, angry gaze met hers. "Your android fed me."

"It's all over you," she pointed out. "He's fed me when I've been sick a few times. He's good at it."

A black eyebrow arched. "Release me and I promise not to kill you."

"Yeah, you're going to take over my shuttle. I heard you the first time. I think I'll pass. Let me call Roid in here and he'll clean you up. I'm so sorry about the mess. I have no idea why this happened."

"I won't eat what he attempted to feed me but he wouldn't stop putting it inside my mouth." His unusually rough voice deepened. "Keep him away from me."

"What's wrong with oatmeal? It's my favorite. I'm sorry you didn't enjoy my breakfast choice but it's morning shift. He's trying to feed you what he thinks a human would want to eat. He's really gentle and wouldn't hurt you." Her gaze flashed over the oatmeal on his skin. "Did you fight him while he spooned it out to you?"

The man growled. "Clean me. It itches."

Clean him? No way, she thought, shaking her head. "I'll get Roid to do that for you."

"I said to keep him away from me," he snarled. His chin tilted up to stare at Arm. "And why is he holding on to this thing still?"

Jill moved closer. "I told him to dig in and hold you so that's exactly what he's doing. He embedded himself into the floor when we escaped from that freighter to keep you from rolling around. That freight table you're on isn't secured to anything and I highly doubt you'd have enjoyed slamming into a wall or worse, toppling over. I figured he could pull double duty by securing you in place and keep you company. He is a great companion if you will allow him to tell you the jokes he knows."

"I want to talk to your male."

"My male?" She blinked. "If you mean my husband, I'm not married."

"I demand to talk to the captain or your commander, whichever term you use, but the male in charge of this ship."

She moved closer and stopped a few feet from him. "You are talking to the person in charge. That's me. This is my shuttle and I'm the only breathing person onboard besides you."

37

Shock crossed his features for a few heartbeats before he hid it. "You're a woman."

She looked down her chest to the cleavage peeking out of her shirt and then grinned, meeting his dark gaze. "Yes, I am. What was your first clue?"

He ignored her attempted humor. "You're human. It is too dangerous for you to travel in space completely alone. Human males are vicious to females."

"Sometimes but I'm not alone. I have Arm, Droid, and Fray."

His attention flickered to Arm's face and then back to Jill's.

"They are androids. They have advanced programming and can adapt and learn." She paused. "Do you want to tell me your name now?"

He glared at her in response.

"Okay." She sighed. "So, what do you eat?" Her focus dropped to his bare chest. "The oatmeal obviously doesn't suit you."

"Your repeated attempts at wit are failures."

"It's a good thing I'm not a comedian then or I'd be out of a job." She turned, moving toward the storage lockers, and yanked open the lower ones, sure that she had cleansing foam containers stored in one of them. The third one she opened contained two bottles of the stuff. She grabbed one and turned, kicking the door closed with her boot. "If you don't want Roid to clean you then I guess I'll have to do it."

The cyborg watched angrily. "Set me free."

"We've been over this. The *Jenny* is all I have and I'm not about to risk losing her to you."

"The *Jenny*?"

"That's the name of this shuttle. It used to belong to my father but he died a year ago and left it to me."

That got some flicker of emotion from him. "I'm familiar with human relationships. Where is your male? You must have one. I demand to speak to him. Males are more reasonable than females."

"Good luck with that. Last I heard, my ex-husband had set up shop on Saturn but he moves around a lot." She stopped near him and studied the nozzle of the container. "And bite your tongue over that last remark. I'd call my ex a lot of things but reasonable would never be one of them. If he were here running this outfit you'd still be on that freighter with those jerks who liked to punch and torture you. He's not one to do anything nice for anyone else unless there is something in it for him." She twisted the cap and a hiss sounded, the small nozzle lifting as it filled. "I lost a trade contact saving your ass so that sure didn't benefit me."

"Why did you do it?"

She lifted her gaze, meeting his. "I told you, I'm a sucker but I'm well aware of my flaws. I always had this thing about rescuing stray animals since I used to be pretty lonely growing up. I guess, now that I'm an adult, I've chosen to save people." She inched closer. "Close your eyes and I'll hose you down. Have you ever used cleansing foam before? You don't want it to get into your eyes. It doesn't hurt but it won't feel good either. It will eat away the oatmeal but not your skin. It melts harmlessly into water."

He watched her silently. She expected him to struggle or attempt something but he didn't move. She bit her lip, glanced down his body, and her gaze froze on his shorts.

"I refuse to breed with you."

Her gaze jerked to his face. "What is up with you and sex? I'm not going to tear your shorts off and attack you."

"You were staring at my groin."

"I'm trying to think of a way to hose you down without getting your shorts wet. I doubt you'd be comfortable with them drying on your body." A horrible thought crossed her mind. "Um, how do you go to the bathroom?"

"You think of this now that I've been on your ship for over twenty-four hours?"

"I'm sorry. I didn't think about it at all. I'm not used to having someone who needs to go." She frowned. "Do you go?" Heat warmed her cheeks as she set the canister down on the floor by him. "Sorry. That's kind of a personal question."

"Your android has assisted me."

She didn't ask how he'd done that and didn't want to know either. "Good. Great." Embarrassment still flowed through her. She should have considered all his needs, not just making sure he had been kept warm and given access to food. "Got any ideas?"

"Release me. You haven't harmed me and for that reason, I'll allow you to live."

"Gee, thanks." She gave him a forced smile. "Aren't you a sweetheart? I guess for a guy who won't even give his name or say thank you for saving his life, that's a huge concession."

"Could you at least release one of my arms? I could clean and feed myself."

"And you could also use your free hand to release the rest of your limbs." She shook her head. "I'm not that stupid. Too softhearted, sure. Flat-out dumb, never."

His eyes narrowed. "Release me."

"Tell me your name."

"If I do, will you release me?"

She shook her head. "Nope. You will take over my shuttle. It's all I have and that's no way to say 'thank you' to me. I did save your life. Has anyone here hit you? No. Those men who had you were going to sell you to fight until death matches."

He frowned, a look of confusion on his strong, handsome features.

"They lock you in a big cage with another fighter or..." her gaze roamed down his impressive body again, "two fighters if the opponent is huge. I'm guessing they would have had a team of men take you on. There's only two ways to get out once they lock you inside one of those cages. You're either killed or you have to be the one who does the killing."

"Truth?"

"No. I just made it up to see that surprised look on your face." She rolled her eyes, shook her head, and stared at him. "Of course it's the truth! Why would I make up that horrible stuff? I wish someone would shut them

41

down but it will never happen. People bet on the fights and they charge people a lot of credits to watch them. It's probably pretty profitable but I can't help but feel sorry for the men fighting. I always suspected that not all of their fighters were there willingly and now I'm sure. The people who run them were going to buy you off that captain and force you to fight."

"I would have refused."

"Then you would have allowed them to beat you to death. I'm certain they don't exactly ask if you want to go inside the cage. You would have been tossed in with people who knew the only way to survive would be to kill you."

His frown deepened. Jill sighed.

"All I can think to do is to cover you with something, tug down your shorts so you're not...exposed. I'll tug them back up once you dry enough not to get them damp. I can do your lower half later."

She turned and spotted some clean rags she used for wiping down spills on the decks. She walked over and grabbed a few then turned to face the glaring cyborg. Her plan didn't seem to amuse him and he definitely didn't appear happy with it.

"Got any other ideas? If you'd allow one of the androids do this, we wouldn't have to worry about embarrassment on either of our parts."

"Your cheeks are pink." He stared at her, continuing to frown.

She blushed more. "I'm not comfortable with this either but that oatmeal has to come off. It's on your lower stomach too. I guess I could hand wash you but that's not something I want to do either. You've already accused me of wanting to rape you. I'm not giving you any ammunition for more of that crap by touching you."

Something in his dark eyes changed, a little of the coolness leaving. "You really do not wish to force sex on me?"

"Hell no!" The idea horrified her.

"You do not enjoy sex with males?" His eyebrow arched as his expression totally relaxed. "I have known females who enjoy touching other females exclusively."

It was Jill's turn to frown. "I'm not into women. I'm not into anyone."

"You have sex with droids?" His focus shifted to Arm and his expression turned to one of horrified shock. His gaze flew back to Jill. "Are they sex droids equipped for sexual relations?"

"No!" Jill had to close her mouth—it had fallen open at that remark. She shook her head. "What is wrong with you? They aren't sex anything. They don't even have those parts or that kind of programming. What is it with you and your obsession over sex?"

"You're human and have urges. It's basic needs."

"Well, I don't have needs, as you put it. I've been there and done that. It wasn't anything worth repeating, especially now that I don't have a man bitching at me until I give in just to shut him up so he doesn't get mad. Sex is for men, not women. Only guys get pleasure from it."

His stunned expression was easy for her to read.

Embarrassment had her clearing her throat. "What?"

"Sex is very pleasurable for women as well as men."

43

"Not in my experience."

"You stated you once had a male."

"Ex-husband. Yeah. He happened to be an asshole and it only became worse when he was in the mood to touch me. I grew up in a remote area where I never got to be around men. When I turned twenty-five my father sent some men to my Aunt's place, ones he approved of, and told me to pick one. I chose my ex because he seemed the nicest out of the bunch. That was a big mistake on my part. I should have picked the scarred freak who resembled a serial killer. I bet he'd have been nicer to me."

"Your male didn't attempt to make sex pleasurable for you when he touched you?"

Jill looked away from his curious, intense gaze. "No. He turned out to be a real bastard. He laughed at me for all those stories I had read about sex. He said I had to be the biggest idiot he'd ever met right before he spun me around, shoved me over the bed, and hurt me the first time we had sex. It was all downhill from there. I was stuck with him for three years until my father realized how bad it had become for me. He saved my ass and got me away from my ex-husband. I never left my Aunt's farm again until last year. My aunt swore sex wasn't all about pain and humiliation but no thanks on ever allowing a guy to touch me after what I survived. The only men I meet are assholes. Would you want the captain of that freighter touching you?" She didn't wait for a response. "Me neither."

"It's a human father's job to protect you. That's what fathers do for their children. He allowed a male to abuse you for that length of time?"

44

Jill walked forward and dropped the large rag over his lap to cover him from ribs to thigh. She refused to look at his face when she shook her head. "We rarely spoke. Every communication he sent put me in danger. My father wasn't well liked and if anyone had known he had a daughter then his enemies would have come after me to get back at him. The first time we spoke, and I told him how miserable it had gotten, he sent men to get me off my ex's ship to return me to my Aunt."

"Are you afraid of sex?" His voice softened.

She glanced at his face. "Let's just say you're totally safe from me molesting you, okay? Ready? I'm going to reach up the sides of your legs and tug down your shorts but you'll remain covered."

He frowned but nodded sharply.

Jill hesitated. She really didn't want to get that close to the intimidating cyborg. She had to lean over him. Her hands shook when she reached under the rag and gripped the bottom of his shorts. Her wrists brushed against hot skin that she tried to ignore.

The cyborg helped her by lifting his hips slightly as she slowly tugged the shorts down. She kept her attention on the line of the rag that dragged down from his ribs to his lower hip region, only stopping when his groin area nearly became exposed. The shorts ended up near his knees and definitely safe from getting wet. She released the material and backed up.

"Okay. That wasn't so hard."

He watched her as she bent and grabbed the foaming-cleanser canister. She checked the nozzle, turned it for use, and then met his gaze.

"Close your eyes and hold your breath. It tingles a bit but in about thirty seconds it will melt into water. Just don't open your eyes. I'm going to get you from head to waist, okay?"

He didn't answer her but he closed his eyes and pulled a deep breath into his lungs. Jill took that for agreement and started to spray him down. White foam coated his head, his face, neck, and she made sure to get his arms too when she covered him in a thick layer of the stuff.

She stepped back and put the canister down, turning away to get more rags. She took her time and then faced him again. The foam melted and with it the oatmeal slid off his muscular, wide chest. She swallowed. Her ex-husband had been pale, overweight, and the only muscles he'd had were those developed from using his insulting mouth to verbally abuse her. She walked closer and waited for the cyborg to open his eyes. He shook his head, lifted his face, and his gorgeous eyes snapped open. They immediately locked on Jill.

"I'll dry you." She shoved one rag under her arm and gripped the second one with both hands. She hesitated and then leaned over him. He had a lot of body to rub down with the dry material. "Just give me a second. I don't want you getting chilled."

He didn't protest when she started at his waist and worked her way up, careful not to touch his skin with hers. She had barely reached his chest when she had to toss away the damp towel and use the second one. She hesitated at his neck, staring at his handsome features.

"If you'll close your eyes I'll dry your face and head."

His intense gaze narrowed but then his eyelids closed. She very gently patted dry his face and his mostly bald head. Her thumb brushed the skin at the top of his head, feeling rough stubble, realizing that he was able to grow hair. She paused, also noting something else about him.

"Are you feeling well?" A horrible thought struck her as she dropped the towel and pressed her palm flat against his forehead. Alarm filled her as it registered how warm he felt. His eyes opened. "You're burning up!"

"I run hotter than humans."

Her hand slid to his cheek and then to his neck. "Are you sure you aren't sick? You really feel feverish. I thought I set the controls to be warm enough to keep you from catching a chill."

He studied her for long moments. "You're touching me."

Her hand jerked away. "Sorry." She lifted her chin and stared at Arm. "Are you monitoring him, Arm?"

Two lighted sensors snapped open and Arm's head adjusted until he'd targeted Jill with them. "Affirmative. His temperature is unchanged from when we rescued our man."

"Our man?" Anger tinged the cyborg's voice instantly while he glared at Jill. "You said you'd free me. You lied?"

"No." She shook her head. "We're going to release you when we reach Hixton Station. He just calls you his man. I told you he'd been designed for military use."

"You said you had him remain with me to keep me company but you lied. He's watching my every move."

"Not really."

"You just asked him if he's been monitoring me."

"Arm is not only a soldier droid but he's a medic. That's what I meant. He monitors all life around him. It's in his programming. He would have scanned you just the way he does me every so often. It's what he does. I just meant had he scanned you for illness recently."

He glared at her. "I don't believe you."

"It's the truth." She shrugged. "It doesn't really matter though. You'll see in a few days when you're standing on Hixton with money to get you back to wherever you came from. Here's some advice though. Stay away from humans." She hesitated. "They aren't nice and you're a rarity, which means you're worth big bucks to traders."

"Are you going to sell me, Jill?"

Hearing him say her name had an odd effect on her. She licked lips that suddenly had gone dry. "No. I stole you to set you free."

"Then do it now."

She took a deep breath. "Even if I were willing to believe you wouldn't kill me outright, I don't trust you not to steal my shuttle. It's not much but it's all I've got. I can't return to Earth."

"Why not? You're human."

She hesitated. "When my father died, I found myself alone on this shuttle with only cargo in the hold and computer records as assets. There wasn't enough fuel to reach Earth. I was stranded out here."

"You traded with those men who had me. Are you going to return to Earth now?"

"No. I can't." She cleared her throat. "The first trade I did to earn money turned really bad and I ended up killing two Earth Government soldiers by accident."

The cyborg frowned. "Why?"

"Because I didn't want to be sold into a whorehouse and when they realized I was alone they tried to grab me to do just that. They not only wanted back the money they'd paid for the cargo I'd sold them but they thought they'd make some bonus bucks off me. I barely made it back to my shuttle alive and then they chased me instead of just letting me fly away. It was before I'd found my guys to help me fool people into thinking I had a live crew who would back me up. I didn't mean to kill anyone but if you haven't noticed, this thing is old. I am not the best pilot since this is my first one I've ever owned and I couldn't outrun them. I was scared enough to steer into an asteroid field. I don't know how I made it out alive. My shuttle took some hits but theirs ended up destroyed. I'm sure I'm wanted on Earth now as a criminal. I can't ever go home."

"So you are alone."

She hesitated. "I have Arm, Fray, and Roid. I'm not alone."

"You have no living beings to rely on?"

She hesitated. "No. I don't. What about you? Do you have a family?" The instant thought of some Mrs. Cyborg had her feeling a little disturbed at the concept. Were there girl cyborgs?

"I have biological links to other cyborgs so the answer would be affirmative. I have family." He paused. "I am not close or in contact with them though."

Chapter Three

"You have no family?" The cyborg seemed genuinely interested.

Jill hesitated. "Do you really want to hear this story?"

"Does it look as if I have anything better to do?"

"No."

She moved closer to him and tugged up his shorts, watching the rag closely. Again he lifted his hips so she could pull them all the way up. After taking a step back, she turned, walked over to an empty crate, and sat down on it. Their gazes locked.

"Have you ever heard of the bloody trader, Big Jim?"

He shook his head. "Someone is actually called that title?"

"I won't lie and say my father didn't earn his reputation because he most certainly did. My Aunt, his sister, never lied to me about what my father did for a living. He had a brutal reputation in space. If anyone gave him any shit or tried to screw him in a deal, they died viciously. That is where the bloody part came in. He actually met my mother after he kidnapped her for ransom since she came from wealth. They fell in love and I came to be. My Aunt said he really worshiped my mother but some of his enemies found out about her. They attacked my father's ship when he was away on a trade. My Aunt Mary managed to smuggle me off the ship while my mother bought us time."

"She fought them?"

Hot tears filled Jill's eyes and she blinked them back. "Yes. I was only a few months old. Aunt Mary jettisoned with me in a life pod and those men didn't come after us because they had my mother. She gave her life to save me."

"That is what a mother should do."

It sounded so cold to her but she nodded. "I guess. My father hunted down every man who was involved and killed them brutally to make an example of what happened to anyone who screwed with something of his. It was so bad he made a name for himself for being a stone-cold killer. He bought a farm on Earth and my aunt raised me there to hide my existence. His enemies either didn't know he ever had a child or they assumed I'd died with my mother. Last year he contacted me and ordered us to go with two men he sent to pick us up. He only had weeks left to live and wanted to see me one last time."

"That is how you got out here in space."

She nodded grimly. "I wouldn't have come if I'd known then what I do now. Big Jim thought he could trust the two men he sent to retrieve me but those assholes betrayed him the second he died. They had sworn a blood oath to him but said that once he stopped breathing all their loyalty died too. They decided one of them would marry me to get their hands on my father's money." She hesitated. "Let me just assure you neither of those guys were anyone you'd want to end up married to and I'm sure I would have had a deadly accident on the forced honeymoon."

"If your father had money, you could have afforded fuel to return you to Earth."

"If I knew where he kept his money, sure. I think it's gone, blown up with his ship. Those men turned on us and my Aunt died saving me. After what happened to my mother she never traveled without weapons. We fought those men in a blaster battle and I ended up injured when I took a hit to my shoulder. I remember her dragging me into the *Jenny*." She waved her hands at the cargo hold. "She leaned over me and said she would make sure they couldn't come after us and she'd be right back. Only she never returned. She had put the *Jenny* on autopilot and she blew up the *Viking*, my father's ship. All of my father's men died with her. I woke up hours later alone, drifting in space, with only the computer logs to tell me what had happened. Aunt Mary had left me a message stating that she could only hold them off if she stayed onboard to stop them from using the life pods to come after me. She said she loved me and to get back home to Earth." She blinked back tears. "Only there wasn't enough fuel."

The cyborg said nothing, just watched her. "So you have no one."

"I told you, I have my androids." Her chin lifted. "And I have the *Jenny*."

"If you release me, I won't harm you or steal your ship. I want access to your communications to contact my friends."

She shook her head. "What if they want to take the ship or sell me? I'm a woman alone in space. I've learned what that means. I never would have survived as long as I have if I didn't lie and pretend to work for Big Jim. Most of the traders I've dealt with are too afraid to mess with me."

"My people won't sell you into slavery. We wouldn't do that with our history."

Regret flashed inside Jill. "I wish I could trust you but I just can't risk it. I've only told you as much as I have because I figure you must be worried about my plans for you. I want you to understand both of us aren't safe from predators in deep space. We have that in common. I also doubt you deal with humans much so my secret should be safe with you. In a few days we'll reach Hixton Station and I'll have Roid obtain you a private room. You can contact your friends from there if you think they can pick you up or you can find accommodations on a shuttle wherever you need to go to meet up with them. It's a well known station with plenty of visitors. I can guarantee you won't be stuck there long and I'll even give you a weapon to defend yourself."

"I want to be freed now."

"And I want to know for sure that you aren't lying to me. I wish I could trust you but I can't." She paused. "You don't trust me either. Until you're standing free on Hixton we both know you half believe this is some kind of trap."

His eyes narrowed consideringly. "Correct."

"Damn straight. I wasn't born yesterday." She took a deep breath. "Are you ever going to tell me your name?"

"Coal."

It surprised her. "Really?"

He frowned. "What is wrong with my name?"

"I just expected something more...I don't know...cyborgish."

"On Earth I was created to work in the mines of the moon and because of my dark eyes the humans called me Coal. It stuck."

"I see." She had to admit that his eyes were nearly black and she could see why they'd tagged him with the name. "It's nice to meet you, Coal."

"I don't feel the same."

"Being here beats being on that freighter."

"No one has abused me on your shuttle."

"And no one will." She stood. "Are you ready to tell me what you will eat? I'm sure you've got to be hungry."

"What are my options?"

She hesitated. "Do you eat sandwiches?" She ticked off her food supplies and then left him there to go prepare lunch.

She wished she could set him free and trust him but she couldn't take that risk. He was a cyborg, something she knew little about, and had no idea of if they held any kind of honor system. If cyborgs had learned from Earth Government then, he definitely couldn't be trusted. As she got two trays ready, she decided to ask Arm if they had any chains onboard that were strong enough to hold Coal without fear of him breaking them. He'd be able to move around, stretch, and walk about if they had them.

Fray met her in the corridor on her way back to the cargo area. "I am on my way to pilot for my shift."

She smiled. "Are you fully recharged?"

"Yes, Jill. I am refreshed."

"Great. Remember to run long distance scans. I'm still worried about that freighter coming after us."

"It would be illogical."

She sighed, not wanting to explain it again after the tough time she'd had with Roid. "Just run the scans. It's an order."

"Of course."

She continued on to the cargo hold, mentally preparing for spending time with Coal. He wasn't what she had expected. She thought he might be similar to her androids but he seemed more human than not with his distrust and questions. She had to admit to enjoying her conversation with him, a nice change from her daily routine. Having someone to talk to again who wasn't programmed for responses made her feel as though he were genuinely interested. The doors automatically slid open when she approached.

Coal's dark gaze fixed on her the second she entered. "Lunch is here."

"I want free."

"I know you do." She walked closer to him and placed both trays on a table Roid had set up next to the freight table Coal lay on. "We've gone over this. I wish I could trust you but I can't take that risk. At worst, you could be lying and kill me. I've gone through a lot over the past year to survive. Before you know it, you'll be able to contact your friends while I'm safely flying away from Hixton Station."

He stared at her with those intensely dark eyes and his full lips curved downward. "I won't hurt you. I do have honor and I give you my word."

"I want to believe you," she stated honestly. "Trust me. It would be great if I could release you." Her gaze fixed on Arm, taking in his damaged face. He'd shut down again, his eyelids closed to hide his eye sensors. "As a cyborg, I bet you're great with electronics." She returned her attention to Coal.

He paused. "If I were fully functional I could have taken control of your androids."

Fear surged through her. "What do you mean?"

He turned his head, twisting it. She saw two scars on the back of his head near the base of his skull. He looked at her again. "Cyborgs usually have implants. Mine were damaged by the females of my species after I repeatedly escaped them. Otherwise I could remotely hack into your androids programming. As for their physical damage I am well versed in adapting to technology." He paused. "I could repair your androids if you free me."

Longing had her feeling tempted but she shook her head. "As much as I really want that, I just can't trust you. There's too much at stake. Can't you just be happy that I stole you from that freighter and from those awful men who abused you? Is it really too much for me to ask you to stop demanding I release you before we reach the station? I really will set you free. This isn't a trap. I have to use logic a lot with my guys so here goes. You're tied down, you can't break free, and I have no reason to lie to you. If I planned on selling you, I'd just tell you that upfront. You couldn't do a thing about it but the real truth is that I'm going to let you go."

They watched each other, both of them frowning. Coal finally inhaled deeply. "I'm willing to trust you on that."

"Great. I'll feed you first and then I'll eat." Her gaze flashed over his chest. "I won't spill anything on you." *I hope*, she thought, not wanting to have to give him another spray down. She gripped his tray and approached him. "Open up."

He ate the soup without trying to bite her or struggle. She fed him bread next and finally the protein shake, which he drank through a straw. When he stated that he'd had enough, she sat on a stool and ate, trying to ignore the silent cyborg who watched her. It felt strange to have someone evaluating her every move but she figured that's exactly what he did. She finished her meal and then gave him her attention again.

"I was thinking about seeing if we could chain you so you have more movement. If we attempt it would you promise to allow it without putting up a fight? It's in your best interest if you agree. I'm sure you'd like to get off that table."

He hesitated. "You're asking me to go against my instincts. At the first opportunity I wish to attempt escape."

He was being honest and she had to admire him for that, even if it wasn't what she wanted to hear. "That's exactly what I'm asking you to do. I really want you to be more comfortable. It bothers me thinking that you—"

"Incoming traffic," Fray's voice stated over the speakers in the room. "It's a large class-C freighter and they are coming fast."

"Oh shit," Jill gasped, standing so fast she suffered a dizzy spell for a second and she stumbled. Her gaze locked with Coal's. "It's got to be the freighter I stole you from. I worried they might not let you go easily."

"Orders?" Fray's voice sounded calm.

Jill was anything but. "Burn fuel and make a run for it." She spun toward the door. "I'm on my way."

"Affirmative." Fray spoke before the speaker clicked off.

"Jill?" Coal growled.

At the door she turned, staring at him with fear. "What?"

"Freighters travel faster than these older-model shuttles."

As if he needs to state the obvious, she thought grimly. "I know. I hoped they wouldn't be able to track us and that they'd been damaged enough that we'd be farther away by the time they made repairs."

"What will happen if they reach us?"

"There will be hell to pay. They'll probably kill me or sell me into a whorehouse if I mange to survive what they do to me first and you'll be on your way to that death match they have planned for you."

He tensed and his arms pulled on the chains that restrained him. "I'm a good pilot. Release me. It's in both our interests if we work together."

She hesitated. "Fray is an excellent pilot. If anyone can fly us away from them, he can." She fled the room and ignored Coal when he called out to her again.

She ran toward the pilot station, certain Fray had followed her orders when the engines struggled to full power and the deck vibrated under her feet. The droid turned his head when she entered the room. He gave her a cold smile or what passed as one.

"I have scanned and there is nowhere to hide. We have the advantage with the smaller ship if we were closer to a planet but we are not. We could have landed on one to wait them out as they are too large to maneuver safely through a planet's atmosphere."

Her gaze lifted to the screens, reading no nearby planets. "Are there any asteroid clusters? They'd never follow us into a stream of them."

"Negative."

Fear notched higher inside her. "Do you have any programming that would help us come up with a solution?"

"Negative. I have run all possible scenarios. It is only a matter of time before they overtake us if we continue to run but our engines are stressed. The probability of explosion increases as they start to overheat." He glanced at something on the control pad. "We are reaching dangerous heat levels already."

She became desperate. "Are there any other ships in range?" She realized asking for help would probably be useless but she had no other ideas.

"Negative."

"Damn," she muttered, sitting down hard in a chair.

Despair filled her. She'd known that stealing the cyborg could cost her very life but she'd hoped they'd gotten away clean. *Obviously not.* She had no idea how the freight carrier had tracked them but they had.

"They are closing fast. Orders?" Fray turned again in his seat to stare at her.

Jill knew it was just a matter of time and probably not much of it before they'd be fired on, the shuttle disabled, and then the freighter would force dock with the *Jenny*. That outraged captain and his crew would come aboard the shuttle.

Jill stood on shaky legs and stepped closer to Fray. "Open communications."

He did and Jill hesitated. "This is the captain of the *Jenny*. I demand you back off immediately."

"You bitch," a familiar voice yelled. "Who the hell do you think you are to steal my property?"

She fought to remember his name. "I'm under orders from Big Jim, Captain Raul. He ordered me to take the cyborg. I apologize for the rudeness but to be blunt, if I don't do what I'm ordered then I'm dead. If you don't cease your pursuit my boss is going to be very angry."

Jill could only pray the captain had more fear of her father's reputation than greed or a sense of getting revenge.

"I don't give a shit. You're dead anyway when I get my hands on you...right after we enjoy having a flesh and blood woman."

The threat came across crystal clear. He'd rape her and pass her off to his crew. She shivered and cut communications, silencing the man who had started to rant and insult her. She glanced at Fray, sadness filling her. She hoped the crew didn't flat-out destroy her androids. She hesitated and then clicked on the shuttle's intercom system.

"Arm, release our man. Unchain him." She paused. "Coal, we're about to be boarded. We can't outrun them and there's nowhere to go. Arm will show you the weapons locker. I'm really sorry I didn't get you to Hixton. I sincerely intended to set you free there. Unfortunately, I can't even blow

60

the *Jenny* and use the explosion to cover us jettisoning away since I don't have a life pod aboard. All I can give you is a fighting chance of not letting them take you alive. Arm, load him up with weapons and take out as many of the men who come aboard as possible." Tears blinded her and emotion choked her voice. "It's been an honor, Arm. Thank you for being my friend." She turned off the microphone and looked at Fray.

The android stared at her as she watched him. Her hand cupped his shoulder. "Thank you for being my friend too, Fray. Can you signal Roid to come to the pilot station? I want both of you here where you'll be safest. They won't blow up this room in a fight since they'll want to raid the captain's safe in the floor under your chair."

"Will you be with us?"

She paused. "No. I'm going to my room. Alert me when they board and then after they reach the living quarters, if you're able, seal it down. I want them trapped in that area. I'm going to fight and take out as many as I can. The hallways are the narrowest there and it will force them to come at me two at a time instead of being able to surround me."

"You will not win this battle."

His cold logic actually soothed her. "Yes, I am aware. I can take some of them out though, before they kill or capture me."

Fray's mouth curved into another cold smile. "We can fight as well."

"You aren't programmed for that."

"I will attempt it."

It touched her that he'd even come up with that solution. "Thanks but no. Just fly to keep them off us for as long as you can."

The doors opened and Jill turned to say goodbye to Roid but instead she gasped as the cyborg stormed into the room. She had known Coal would be intimidating when free and standing. The sight of nearly six and a half feet of muscular male in just a pair of baggy shorts, muscles rippling and guns strapped around his hips in a weapons belt had her upgrading her opinion to terrifying.

Coal's gaze pinned her where she stood and then he jerked his attention to the pilot's seat. "Move, android," he growled. "I'm not going to allow anyone to board us."

Fray turned his head to peer at Jill. "Orders?"

She couldn't look away from Coal. He shot her a dark glare. "Tell him to move before I toss him out of that seat."

"Let him have the helm, Fray," she whispered.

Coal lunged forward to drop into the vacant seat the instant Fray moved. "Strap in."

She dropped into the nearest chair and reached for a belt. "You heard him, Fray. Hang on." She hesitated. "The gravity stabilizers are old so if you—" She gasped in surprise, her words lost when Coal suddenly turned the shuttle violently.

"They are bad," he grumbled when the ship tilted dangerously, shaking violently.

"Yes. They can't adjust to sudden movements as you just realized."

Her attention landed on the screens and she realized he flew directly at the freighter instead of away from it. Her mouth opened but no sound came out. Shock and fear held her totally immobile while she silently watched the huge ship growing even larger.

"Impact warning," Fray calmly stated.

"We're not hitting it...but close. They can fly faster but we can maneuver better." Coal's deep voice sounded unnaturally calm under the dire circumstances.

"What are you doing?" Jill found the ability to speak over her terror.

"They can't pursue us if they are damaged." His hands flew across the controls and the sounds of the *Jenny's* weapons firing drowned out anything else he might have said.

He flew right under the belly of the freighter, tearing open holes as explosions filled the screen with bright flashes of destruction. Jill's fear turned to pure astonishment. She'd never thought to attack the much larger ship, especially with her older shuttle, not believing she could do that much damage. Coal proved her wrong as he steered them up the back of the freighter and took more shots, blowing up their thrusters.

The large freighter's engines died when the lights of their thrusters cut out. Jill watched as it shuddered in space, the lights flickering on the entire ship, and then Coal flew the *Jenny* away, putting distance between the two ships. Jill said nothing but her thoughts were jumbled. Coal had saved them.

He finally turned his seat to face her, full lips curving into a grim frown. "Hand over control of your droids or I'll harm them. I'd hate to do it, considering I am aware they have deep value to you. I want full control of them and for them to ignore your requests to them. Do it."

She gaped at him.

"Now, Jill. I want absolute control of them or I will take them out." His hand lowered to one of the weapons strapped to his hips.

Dread balled inside her. Not only did the cyborg have his freedom now but he wanted to command not only her ship but her friends. "Fray?" She paused, blinking back tears. "This is Coal. He owns you now. You are to follow all of his orders from this moment forward and none of mine. Verify order."

Fray hesitated. "Order confirmed." He turned his head to glance at Coal. "Orders, Coal?"

"The rest of them as well, Jill." Coal's fingers tightened on the weapon.

She fought the urge to order Arm to come to her rescue but she had a feeling that Coal could fight. She didn't want him to destroy her androids. She slowly reached for the ship intercom system and turned it on shipwide.

"This is Jill. Arm and Roid, your new owner is the man down. You are to follow all of his orders from now on and none of mine. His name is Coal. Verify order." She turned off the com but knew they had heard her. She stared silently at the cyborg in charge of everything she cared about. "Are you going to kill me now?"

His frown deepened. "No. Stand up." He rose to his feet, facing her, and released his weapon.

She hesitated.

"Now."

Her hands shook when she unfastened her belt and rose on trembling legs. He closed the distance between them. Jill had to tilt her chin up to focus on his grim features. He stood over a foot taller than she did.

64

He stopped in front of her. "I won't harm you. You saved my life and I know that."

Jill gasped when he suddenly crouched, two large hands shot out to grip her waist, and he jerked her body forward. Her hip hit a broad shoulder and then the world turned upside down. A dizzy spell gripped her when he quickly straightened to his full height.

He spun around with Jill dangling over his shoulder. One hand gripped the small of her back to keep her bent in place while his other arm locked behind her thighs. Coal paused by the door.

"Fray, I have set a course. Follow it and alert me if any ships come within range. You have the helm."

"Yes, Coal," Fray stated calmly before reclaiming the pilot seat.

Jill stared at the deck, some feet below her. The cyborg walked quickly out of the room. He seemed to know how to go directly to the crew quarters. He confirmed that when he spoke as they reached it.

"Which is yours?"

She paused.

His hold on her tightened. "Answer me."

"The captain's quarters are straight ahead. I converted the other three rooms for the droids to use to recharge."

Coal stopped when he carried her into her room and seemed to study the space. The silence between them became so absolute that she heard every breath he took. He moved suddenly and Jill cried out when he bent without warning, released her, and she found herself flung onto her back on top of her bedding. She stared up at the cyborg, who looked huge and terrifying.

"You're my prisoner now. Don't move while I find something to restrain you. If you fight I will harm you." His eyelids narrowed dangerously. "Do you understand me?"

She could only nod. Without weapons she stood no chance of winning a fight between them.

"Good." He took a deep breath. "I've never been on this side of things but as someone who has spent a lot of time being a captive, I give you my word, I won't abuse you." To her shock the cyborg suddenly laughed, his dark eyes seeming to twinkle. "I admit I enjoy being the one in control for the first time."

Chapter Four

Jill struggled against the leggings that held her wrists to the headboard but they had no give in them. Frustration and fear were two emotions she had grown accustomed to in the past few hours since Coal had tied her and left her alone in the room.

The doors opened and the cyborg entered her quarters. He had located a pair of pants that were a little small judging by the snug way they stretched across his hips and thighs, the material enhancing his muscular his legs. His chest remained bare. He paused at the end of her bed. He'd shaved his head, the stubble that had begun to show was now just a memory.

"The freighter isn't following us and I doubt it will be able to travel for a very long time."

"Good." The last thing she needed would be another run-in with them. "What are you going to do with me and my droids?"

He cocked his head slightly, watching her for a long moment. "I've set a course to take us to the last location where I know my people's ships were. I don't want to risk communications. We are closer to Earth than I wish and the probability is high that they might overhear my transmission."

Cyborgs had ships, which meant there were more of them. She digested that information. "What are you going to do with us if you find your friends?"

"I'll release you and your shuttle."

Relief swept through her. "Thank you." She wanted to believe him but part of her remained leery. "Do you promise?"

"I'll tell you what you told me. You're my prisoner, I am in control, and I have no reason to give you false hope. I could do anything to you that I wish but I don't want to harm you."

"I didn't say it that coldly."

An eyebrow arched. "I am not you."

"How are my droids?"

"Fine." He paused, his features relaxing. "You have a lot of spare parts stored in your cargo hold. Why didn't you fix them? Most of the supplies are there if you'd only inventoried what you possessed."

"I don't know how. I had to teach myself to pilot and I did replace their damaged eye sensors. I just couldn't find matching ones. They aren't blind. I'm kind of proud of that."

"I wouldn't be. You did a bad job. The color is adjustable. They have fully functioning vision now, matching colored lenses, and no more short circuits."

She relaxed. "You really fixed them?"

"I enjoy working while I think."

"Thank you." She meant it, knowing he hadn't had to do it.

He shrugged. "It needed to be done. Your entire shuttle is in bad shape. It will take us days to reach our destination and in the meantime I have made a list of repairs to tackle."

"Really?" A rush of appreciation filled her. "Thank you. That's so nice."

His posture straightened even more. "You saved my life and didn't mistreat me. I checked your computer logs and you were headed for Hixton Station just the way you stated. I also talked with the droids while I worked on them. You had no reason to deceive them and they were certain you meant to release me upon arrival. They state that you are honest and do not tell them lies. I decided, after reviewing the facts, that you need to be rewarded. You admitted to losing a financial opportunity by removing me from the freighter. While I don't have money to pay you, I do have expertise." He paused. "I've decided to repair your ship, your droids, and you."

She felt gratitude right up until that last word. "Me? I'm not hurt."

"You're afraid of males and believe sex is one-sided. That's a flaw on your part. Your male harmed you."

"My ex-male and I'm fine. I don't want to hear a lecture on it again. I also don't want to date anyone in the future. It's not a defect if it's not a problem."

"I am not going to talk to you." He reached for the front of his pants. "I am going to show you pleasure."

Jill gaped at him, her mind trying to make sense of his words while dread rolled through her. Coal tore open his pants to reveal—

Her gaze jerked upward and she locked her full attention on his face, refusing to glance down at the dusky, hairless skin he'd revealed under his navel. "You're not wearing underwear."

"I was fortunate to find pants that barely fit. The males who discarded the clothing I found were much smaller than I." He bent, stepping out of the pants. "Do not fear me."

"Stop," Jill ordered. "I'm not flawed or damaged. Put the pants back on." Her gaze nearly strayed downward to his groin area when he straightened, knowing he stood there naked, but she kept her gaze locked with his by sheer force alone, ignoring her curiosity. "I don't want fixed."

"I reviewed your medical history. You told the truth when you stated Arm is a medic model as well as a defensive android and he has detailed scans on you." Coal put a knee on the mattress, the bed dipping from his weight near Jill's feet. "I calculated your cycles and now is a safe time for you to have intercourse."

"What?" She gasped.

"You're not ovulating." Coal paused, frowning at her. "I don't wish to impregnate you. I am a unique cyborg by having active, healthy sperm. It's why female cyborgs forced me into being a breeder while they kept me in captivity."

"I don't want you to touch me. I don't want to have sex with you. Just stay back, Coal."

He watched her silently for long moments before he spoke. "I don't see fear. You appear angry."

"You're threatening to force sex on me, the thing you feared I'd do to you. I am angry. I didn't hurt you and molesting me would just be wrong."

"I won't harm you."

Jill snorted. "Sure. Right. Put your pants on. I don't want this."

"You honestly believe intercourse is painful."

"It is." Fear inched up her spine but she tried to mask her emotions and not show it. Her ex-husband had gotten more turned on when he knew he'd terrified her. "Please don't touch me, Coal. I saved your life."

"We'll start with the basics." He hesitated. "Don't fight me."

Jill jerked up her legs to her chest and kicked out with both feet together, aiming for Coal's wide chest. Her boots never made contact. Large, strong hands grabbed her ankles instead and took the force, slowing her momentum until he held her legs immobile inches from his body. His frown deepened.

"I ordered you not to fight me."

"Go fuck yourself if you want to get laid."

His eyes narrowed as he stared down at her. "This isn't about my pleasure, it's about yours."

"Then put your pants back on. That would make me really happy."

He sighed, blowing out a deep breath. "Relax."

"Leave me alone."

"You're making things more difficult."

"I saved your life. I didn't have to steal you from that freighter. I could have left you there to be beaten and sold. You said you were grateful." She tried to find the guy's conscience. "You said you were forced to have sex with women. You don't want to do that to someone else, do you?"

"We don't need to have actual intercourse but I will fix your fear of men touching you and show you that pleasure isn't one-sided." His hands

71

shifted their hold on her ankles, lifting her legs higher until her bottom rose from the bed. "I hoped you would welcome the lesson."

"I don't." She wiggled but he didn't release her.

Coal shifted his hold again, using his thumb to wrap around one of her ankles and his fingers curled around the other one, holding both together with one hand. His free hand tore off her boots. He tossed them behind him, the sound of them hitting the floor was loud inside the room.

Jill struggled and twisted when he reached around her and unfastened her pants. It didn't do any good when he got them open and tugged them upward, baring the lower half of her body. He took not only her pants but her panties when his fingers hooked into the waistband of both.

"Damn you," she panted. "Stop!"

"I'm much stronger than you are. Fighting is a waste of your energy."

"I saved you," she raged.

"And I'm repaying you."

"You're really screwed up if this is the thanks I get."

He paused, her pants bunched at her knees. A frown marred his features as their gazes locked together. "I am flawed." Broad shoulders shrugged. "Tell me something I don't know."

"I don't want this."

"I don't have money to repay you. I owe you for saving my life."

"Then let me go. You're in command of the *Jenny* and my droids. You're a tank on legs and I know fighting you would be flat-out stupid. I'm willing to believe that you're going to let me go when we find your friends

72

and that you'll turn everything back to my control. You can fix stuff and that's payment enough, okay?"

Coal still hesitated. "I want to fix you as well. I know women's bodies and while you're not a cyborg female, I feel confident that I'm capable of giving you pleasure. The least I can do is right the wrong done to you by a male."

She knew that he was completely serious and meant what he said. He thought touching her would fix what her ex-husband had done. The truth showed clearly in his slightly confused expression. She twisted hard, trying again to break free. Regardless of his motives, she didn't want to have sex.

"I'll make a deal with you."

Jill stopped struggling. "What kind of deal?"

"Let me pleasure you at least and if you don't enjoy what I do then I will stop."

"I don't want you to touch me."

"I'm going to but I am willing to negotiate the terms by offering a reasonable solution with a deal."

"What if I say no?"

"You'll continue to fight me and make it more difficult for me to fix you."

"And if I agree and don't like what you do to me?"

"I'll stop."

"Okay, stop. I'm not enjoying this."

"I haven't begun yet." His dark gaze flashed his annoyance.

73

Jill glared at him. He continued to frown at her, unmoving, until her legs began to hurt from his hold on her ankles.

"This isn't real comfortable."

He eased her ass back down onto the bed and released her ankles. She pulled her legs down, trying to cover her exposed lower region but Coal used it to his advantage, tearing her panties and pants the rest of the way down her legs. He tossed them behind him. Jill gasped and put her heels against her bottom, her knees drawn up, and locked together to cover her sex while she glared at him over the top of them.

"Spread your thighs for me."

"No."

"Give me five minutes of access to your body and if you want me to stop after that time, I will. That's fair."

"Fair would be you untying me and handing me a weapon to even out the odds between us."

The grin that flashed on his features changed his entire look from intimidating to kind of cute in Jill's opinion. She tried not to notice. The guy knelt on the end of her bed, watching her.

"That isn't going to happen." He looked smug.

"Neither is you touching me."

"It is."

"No."

Coal's grin faded. "I swear not to enter you if you give me five minutes of not fighting and doing as I ask. What do you have to lose?"

"I—"

He cut her off. "You have everything to gain if you agree. I will release you if you want me to stop after five minutes. I'll free you from the bed and allow you to roam your quarters after I search through it to make sure there are no hidden weapons for you to use against me."

"That's not fair."

"Life isn't fair. You're an adult female. This shouldn't be a new fact for you to learn." He arched a dark eyebrow. "Decide."

"That's blackmail. What are you going to do if I don't agree?"

"I will keep you tied on the bed and keep trying to get you to agree to allow me to touch you until you realize pleasure is possible."

"I really don't like you," she admitted.

"I believe I could make you change your mind about that."

"Has anyone ever called you a bastard before?"

"Since I don't have a mother and wasn't given birth to—no."

"Here's a first for you then. You're a total bastard."

He had the nerve to chuckle. "Do you agree?"

Jill wanted to scream in frustration. The big cyborg could force sex on her and she wouldn't be able to stop him. So far he hadn't hurt her and she believed that wasn't his intention. Sometimes her droids had set ideas in their programming and it took her a long time to make them understand an error. Perhaps Coal had a glitch in his thinking that had him believing what had been done to her could be easily fixed, as if showing her

75

something once would make years of misery disappear. He'd said he had implants and his brain might be more computer-like than she had guessed.

They studied each other as she chewed on her lower lip. She assessed that he looked pretty determined. If cyborgs and androids were anything similar, he had this course of action firmly set in his brain. She took careful breaths. He wouldn't hurt her, she saw no cruelty in his gaze, and hoped her instincts were right.

"Do I have a choice? I want free."

"Open your thighs wide for me."

She hesitated. "What guarantee do I have that you won't force yourself on me? You might say you won't enter me but—" She gasped.

Coal pushed her thighs open. "If I wanted to force myself inside you I could and you wouldn't be able to stop me. Is my point made?"

Fear made Jill's heart race. She nodded, unable to speak. She hadn't expected him to do that. He had her legs pinned open and spread wide.

"I've only let a doctor see me this way."

He shook his head. "Your male was stupid if he didn't ask you to spread your sex open for your mutual stimulation."

She couldn't exactly argue with Coal over his assumption since anyone willing to badmouth her ex had to be right. The hands gripping her knees weren't painful but he had a good hold on her that prevented it when she tried to shift her legs closed. Her gaze lowered and her mouth parted in shock. Fear came rushing back as she stared at the naked, aroused cyborg and his definitely massive hard-on.

"Your fear isn't necessary, Jill."

"You're big all over." Her gaze refused to leave that darker-hued, hard cock pointing right at her as the cyborg held her thighs spread open. "Too big."

Coal followed her gaze to his sex and then lifted his head to frown at her. "If we progress to actual intercourse, I won't harm you. Women's bodies are designed to stretch. It's just a matter of entering slowly to give you time to adjust to my size."

"Easy for you to say. You're not the one facing having something that size shoved where the light doesn't shine."

He had the nerve to laugh. Jill glared at him. Coal smiled as he inched closer to her. His gaze lowered to the vee of her thighs and his mouth parted, his tongue swiping his full lips to wet them.

"You have very little hair for a human."

"I thought you said you only know cyborg women." Jill tried to distract herself from the fact that he studied her pussy very closely. No one but her doctor ever had. Not even her ex had put her under scrutiny the way Coal did. He seemed fascinated, judging by his expression. "You don't have any hair down there so I'm assuming they don't either."

"They either have no hair at all or a lot of it." He cocked his head. Dark brown eyes rose to meet hers. "Is your hair pattern shaped similar to an arrow?"

A blush heated Jill's cheeks. "It gets really boring onboard sometimes, okay? Stop giving me that look. I don't like a lot of body hair and when I use the hair remover wand I tend to make patterns sometimes." She paused. "That's not weird."

"If you say so. It is attractive. Our time starts now and I'll stop in five minutes if you still wish me to."

He called her muff attractive. Jill frowned but then she realized the time ticked down. As long as he examined her he wasn't doing anything else. She relaxed. She'd just talk and stall him until his five minutes had elapsed.

"I could tell you how to make patterns with the wand."

Something flickered in his eyes. "I know you could. Tell me after my four minutes and fifty seconds have elapsed."

"Damn!" *So much for my plan,* she thought. Jill tensed when he leaned over, his face hovering close to her skin. His intention became clear as hot breath fanned across her inner thighs. Her eyes widened and her mouth dropped open. "You can't!"

He paused, giving her an amused smile and an eyebrow arched. "I can't what?"

"You know." A deeper blush spread across her cheeks. "I read fiction files with sex in them and you can't do that. I'd assumed you'd want to touch but not put your face there."

"Why not?"

"It's um…well, unsanitary." She nodded, going with that.

He had the audacity to laugh. "That's the best excuse you can pull from your mind? No wonder you don't know sexual satisfaction if you wouldn't allow your male to touch you as he wished."

"He never tried that."

Coal sighed, blowing more hot air over her thighs and pussy. "Pathetic."

"I am not."

"I was speaking about your male. Shut up, Jill." He frowned. "Relax and give it a try. You will enjoy it. I have a vast amount of experience at this."

"They forced you to do that too?" Her mouth dropped open. "I thought only men tried to make women go down on them."

Anger tightened his handsome face. "Your male forced you to your knees?"

"He tried a few times but it didn't work out for him. It seems we have a lot in common." She refused to admit it but bad memories flashed through her mind of her ex-husband yelling at her and attempting to do just that until she's threatened to kill him in his sleep.

A deep growl came from Coal's throat. "It wasn't all force with the females who held me." He took another deep breath. "Once they damaged the chips inside my head that allowed me to close off my physical responses I found sexual enjoyment even though I wasn't willing at first to be a breeder. If someone touches your body in the correct manner, the need for sexual gratification becomes intense. You will participate in the act."

"I don't see that happening."

"You're wasting time, Jill. Silence."

Jill closed her lips firmly, shooting a glare at him. "Fine." She threw her head back, staring at the beam along the ceiling. "I can't stop you but I just want you to know I'm really uncomfortable with this. I'm counting down the seconds until I can tell you to stop."

79

"You do that." He sounded amused. "I'll do this."

Warm hands adjusted their hold, sliding from her knees to her inner thighs, holding her open wider but gripping her inches from her pussy. The mattress shifted as Coal's big body changed position, and to Jill's shock, two thumbs spread her vaginal lips apart to expose her inner sex to his view. She squeezed her eyes closed and tensed, hoping it wouldn't be as uncomfortable as she suspected.

"You're pink." Surprise was an easy emotion to hear coming from him.

"What color should I be?"

He cleared his throat. "White or a very light gray."

"Really? Cyborgs are that color down there?" Jill conceded this had to be the strangest conversation she'd ever had.

"Yes."

Jill opened her mouth to ask him another question, hoping to use up more time, but then shock assailed her as a hot, thick tongue made contact with her clit. She tensed, the sensation freezing the air inside her lungs. A soft growl came from Coal and then his full lips locked around her clit.

Her eyes sprung open wide as he started to suckle on her. His tongue moved back and forth rapidly at the same time. Raw pleasure coursed from between her spread thighs straight to her astounded brain. She gasped in air when she realized she'd totally stopped breathing and as air filled her lungs again, her eyes closed.

Her body tensed and she tried to wiggle away from the intense attack on her pleasure center. Coal's hands held her firmly in place as if he'd bound her immobile. It heightened the ecstasy each lash of his tongue gave Jill. A moan passed her lips.

Coal growled louder, sending vibrations through her clit right to her belly, which tightened in response. Her muscles strained as her body tensed more and she realized her heels dug into the bed. It horrified her a bit that she seemed to be pressing upward against his mouth instead of trying to jerk away. The fire that burned throughout her body grew hotter until she knew sweat beaded her skin. She wasn't breathing anymore so much as panting loudly.

Just when she thought she'd die from the overload of rapture, the cyborg pulled his mouth away. Shock gripped her for a second time as she lay there trying to catch her breath, aching for something she was certain would be sexual release.

"Look at me," Coal demanded in a husky voice.

Jill forced her eyes open to stare down her body at him. She couldn't speak, had no words, and fought the confusion in her mind.

"The five minutes is up. Do you want me to stop?" His eyes appeared black and his features had darkened slightly, his normal skin tone apparently flushed. "I keep my word and we made a deal." He paused. "Let me give you pleasure. Allow me to finish."

I've lost my mind, she could finally think. Her body ached, hurt actually, especially where his mouth had just been. Her clit throbbed painfully and her belly quivered. She could feel wetness trickling down the seam of her pussy.

"Jill," his voice deepened. "Let me continue."

Her mouth opened but no words came out.

"You should see how beautiful you look." His thumb shifted and rubbed her swollen clit.

Jill gasped, the sheer intensity of that light touch had her fighting back a moan.

"Your increased breathing has made you pinker and your blue eyes have darkened with passion." Coal rubbed a slow circle over the swollen bud with the pad of his thumb. He inhaled. "I could make a meal out of you. You taste as good as you smell. Have you ever had a male fill you with his tongue?"

Nope, she thought, still unable to speak.

"I know the answer since no male has done this to you before." His thumb slid lower and slowly breached her pussy, entering her gently.

Jill threw her head back, moaning, surprised at how incredibly wonderful it felt to have his thick digit penetrating her. There was no pain, just sheer euphoria as some of the aching need inside her eased. Her hips tilted on disobedience of her will, helping him slide in deeper.

"Coal!" She wasn't sure what she wanted, what she meant to say, but only his name passed her lips.

"That sounds to be a yes to me." He rasped the words before his thumb withdrew and he entered her again, this time with one of his fingers. He adjusted his hold on her until one hand kept her vaginal lips spread while he used his thumb to press against her clit. He started to pump his finger in and out of her pussy.

Jill clawed at the headboard, her fingers frantic to find anything to grip. Sensations swamped her, too much for her to take in or even attempt to control. She'd never experienced anything that strong, that extremely delightful, and then she screamed when the climax gripped her. Her body shook with each explosive shock of release that flashed until she nearly lost consciousness.

The first thing she became aware of had to be her rapid breathing. She wondered how many seconds had passed, praying it had only been that short of a time before she came around, and then moaned again when Coal slowly withdrew his finger from her still-quivering pussy. She forced her eyes open and met a pair of totally black, angry-looking eyes.

It baffled her—the evident rage coming from Coal. She just stared at him when he rose up to his hands and knees, managing to avoid her now limp, spread legs on the mattress. He growled words she didn't understand, spoken too softly for her to hear. She couldn't look away from him as he backed off her bed, stood at the end of it, and continued to glare down at her.

She glanced down Coal's body and saw his cock still hard, actually twitching to a heartbeat tune of its own, and then he spun around, presenting her with a beefy, bare ass.

"I was incorrect. You're very tight and I fear I'll hurt you. I'm sorry. I was too sexually stimulated. I need to cool off before I can trust myself not to harm you."

Jill watched in mute shock as the naked cyborg stormed out of her quarters, leaving her still tied to her bed, minus her pants and still reeling from what he'd done to her. A full minute later, she shifted her leg, straightening it, just lying there trying to catch her breath. Her foot touched a wet spot on the edge of her bed and she lifted her head to see what it was.

"Oh shit," she sighed, understanding why he'd fled.

* * * * *

Coal punched the exterior bulkhead in the hallway when the door to Jill's quarters slid shut. Humiliation and embarrassment gripped him. He welcomed the pain that shot up his arm from where his fist had impacted the unforgiving metal. Anger also burned through him. The female cyborgs had damaged him in more ways than just taking his ability to remote link to computers. They'd damaged his mind until he had a hard time controlling his physical responses.

He turned his head, staring at the door to the captain's quarters, and wondered what Jill thought of him now. Her beautiful blue eyes staring at him with such passion would be a memory he'd never forget. Maybe she wouldn't know that he'd come just from hearing her and tasting her. When her muscles had clamped down around his finger and he'd felt her release, he'd lost all control with the scent of her drowning his senses. Just brushing his cock against her comforter had done him in. He'd come as if he were an untried human male who'd just had sex for the first time.

His shoulders slumped. He flexed his throbbing hand and glanced at it, noting blood smeared across two knuckles. *I can't even control my own temper*, he admitted silently. His eyes closed and he took deep, calming

84

breaths. He opened them and walked down the corridor after he regained control of his raging emotions.

How can I face her? He had no answer to the questions that plagued him. *I've offered to fix her yet I can't even repair myself.*

He entered the cargo hold and frowned at Arm. The droid's sensor eyes opened and his human-like features shifted into a simulation of a smile.

"Hello, Sir."

"Shut down. I'm going to use one of those cleansing canisters and I don't want you watching me. I don't even want to see me right now."

Arm hesitated and then followed orders. The light turned off in his sensors and he went completely still. Coal envied the droid his total control as he jerked open the cabinet where Jill had stored the canister when she'd cleaned him. He knew he'd have to face her soon. She'd need to eat dinner. He'd be damned if she suffered just because he'd had a really embarrassing and frustrating moment in front of her.

Chapter Five

The smell of food woke Jill. When she opened her eyes, she noticed a much calmer Coal standing inside her quarters. He'd donned another pair of ill-fitting pants, stood shirtless just inside the door, and held a tray. He didn't say a word when he placed it on the only table in the room.

"Could I use the facilities? I'd also like not to be naked from the waist down."

The cyborg turned to face her. "I planned to untie you."

Embarrassment heated her cheeks when she noticed the way Coal's gaze ran over her body, hesitating on her bare thighs with an intensity that she couldn't miss. He cleared his throat when he closed the distance between them.

"I apologize for my abrupt departure before."

Jill wasn't sure what to say as he carefully untied her wrists. It wasn't all right. He'd left her half naked and confused by his anger. That had been the most mind-blowing experience of her life and he'd just stalked out afterward. She sat up when he freed her, tugged her shirt down to cover her lap, and started to rub her wrists.

"Do they hurt?" He slowly sat on the edge of the bed, their gazes finally meeting. He held out his hands. "Let me see them."

"They are fine." She wasn't sure letting him touch her would be a good idea even if she doubted he'd hurt her.

"You're angry."

"No." She debated her words carefully. "I'm confused and not sure what we're supposed to say to each other now. I've never…"

"Never what?" He studied her expression carefully. "Been tied down?"

"Oh, I've been tied up lots of times. My ex-husband did that regularly when he feared I'd try to run away. My father would have killed him if I'd run from him and something bad had happened to me while I was in his care. I just don't know how to act around you."

"He abused you by restraining you to force sex acts upon your body. Something bad did happen to you." Anger deepened Coal's voice.

"He never considered the things he did to me as mistreatment as long as he didn't beat me up. His idea of abuse would have been if I'd managed to escape our quarters and some of his men raped me. He knew my father would have gutted him if another man ever touched me."

"I could track him down and kill him."

Jill grinned. "You look serious."

He blinked. "I am."

"Darren isn't worth it."

"That is his name?"

"I tend to go with asshole but yeah. That's what his mother put on his birth certification." She shrugged. "Besides, I have a feeling my father made him pay. I told you he earned that bloody title but he did allow the asshole to live."

"If you were mine, I'd protect you better than your father did."

Her smile died as she realized his utter sincerity. "Thank you." It touched her that he meant it. "If I were yours, I'd appreciate it."

Coal glanced away and then looked back. "We should discuss what happened. I'm damaged. It is not your fault that I failed in the lesson I wanted to teach you. It has been a long time since I touched a female—not since I gained my freedom, and the situation greatly stimulated me sexually. You're very attractive to me. I've also never had a female under my total control and I enjoyed it too much."

Jill's mind froze. Most guys in her limited experience with them wouldn't ever talk about it if they had an embarrassing moment. They'd just pretend it never happened. She wasn't sure what to say so she shrugged.

"It's all right."

"It isn't. I wish to fix you yet I'm severely physically damaged myself. I plan to attempt it again only this time I will make sure that incident isn't repeated." He hesitated before reaching into his pocket and withdrawing a round, green band of rubber. "I downloaded some information on the computer. This will help."

"A rubber vent seal? I know what that is. I had to fix a ruptured one when it annoyed me by whistling from a gap between the vent and the opening for it."

"The specifics are close enough to stimulate a cock ring."

Jill knew her mouth dropped open while she gaped at him.

"It will help me keep an erection longer without early ejaculation."

Jill had no words.

"I've shocked you." He shoved the rubber ring back inside his pocket. "I let you down before but I won't again."

"It's not a big deal." She nodded. "Really. Let's just drop this."

"For the time being, we can. Use the facilities while I search your room for hidden weapons and then we'll eat." He hesitated. "Afterward we'll work on your fear of males again."

She forced herself to move. She fled to the small room in the corner, closing the door behind her. She leaned against it, staring at the foam-cleanser unit before she forced her body to move.

She washed her hands and face and brushed her teeth last. She stared at the closed door. He stood on the other side. She was uncertain of what to do and didn't want to leave the small room.

"Jill?" He tapped on the door. "Do not attempt to attack me."

"I won't."

"You closed the door."

"I had to use the facilities."

"Come out."

She hesitated and then reached for the handle. The big cyborg stood there blocking her exit. She attempted to swallow down her anxiety.

"I didn't want you watching me while I attended to my needs."

"Understood. I do not enjoy being watched either while I perform private acts." He stepped back. "Come eat. I prepared food."

Her stomach rumbled at the mere mention of eating. The smell of food penetrated her senses. She slowly eased around him to perch on the edge of the bed, the only place to sit in her quarters. She moved slowly, hoping Coal would realize she wasn't stupid enough to physically assault him.

Coal hesitated and then retrieved the tray. He carried it to the bed, sat near her, and placed the food between them. He waved a hand at her plate.

"Proceed."

She only hesitated a second before reaching for the sandwich. The filling was synthetic protein, but he served it warm instead of cold. The silence in the room grew a little uncomfortable while she chewed the food. She ventured a look at him when she swallowed.

"Good?" He held his own sandwich inches from his lips, studying her closely.

"Yes. Thank you."

"I promise to take very good care of you while you remain in my custody. I'm certain you are worried about your future but there is no need. I plan to locate my people, restore control of your shuttle and droids to you, and leave peacefully when they dock with us."

Staring into his eyes, she hoped the honesty and openness she saw wasn't just wishful thinking on her part. "Okay. Thank you."

"You saved me. I know humans can be devious and cruel but I'm a cyborg. I know right from wrong and I'm indebted to you."

"I'm glad to hear you say it."

"I'm still going to fix you, Jill."

Her heart missed a beat. "There's no need. You showed me that not all touches hurt."

Anger tightened his mouth before he took a bite, chewed. He watched her with a hooded gaze until she looked away, concentrating on her food instead. They ate in silence. Coal finished before she did and he stood, staring down at her.

Jill sipped her drink, purposefully ignoring him, and avoided lifting her chin, though she could feel him watching her, waiting. Nervousness made her hands tremble. He planned to touch her again, had admitted that, and she didn't know how to react. He hadn't hurt her before, the exact opposite in fact, and she admitted to being a little curious now that her fear wasn't present.

"You're stalling." His voice was soft and sounded amused.

"Yes." There was no reason to lie. "I don't know what you want from me, Coal."

"Look at me."

She looked up at him as she returned the drink to the tray. Coal's dark, intense eyes were locked on her face. He reached for the waistband of his pants and she lowered her focus to watch his fingers work the front opening.

"I will not hurt you. This is going to be about learning pleasure."

He wiggled his hips slightly to bare more of his body when his pants lowered. It fascinated her as his skin was revealed. A few inches more and she held her breath as his cock sprang free from the material. She stared at his large, erect sex, which pointed straight up at her. It amazed her that something that size could defy gravity. This time she wasn't afraid of him.

"What frightens you about males?"

She swallowed hard. "I told you, I've been hurt." She didn't expand her explanation, figuring he could guess from what she'd already told him about her ex.

"I really could track him down and kill him for you if you were to ask it as payment from me for rescuing me from the freighter."

"Don't tempt me." It shocked her when she smiled, amused at the image of how Darren would react if he ever ran into the terrifying cyborg. She realized she should be running for another room to try to hide from the man who pushed his pants down his thighs and stepped out of them. Instead she said, "He enjoyed fear. It turned him on more."

"I don't want that." Coal straightened, stood motionless, allowing her to study every inch of him if she dared. "What will make you less afraid of me? You may touch me."

The idea of reaching out to put her hands on him had her lacing her fingers together in her lap. Curiosity tempted her to actually do it.

"I won't attack you. I won't get so excited that I harm you. Touch me. Perhaps that will make you more comfortable with the sight of my body." He hesitated. "I know my size is intimidating but I'd never use it against you to cause any pain."

An emotion flashed in his eyes but she caught it. She just wasn't sure why he felt vulnerable. She had a lifetime of feeling that way—she recognized that look.

"This is insane."

He moved slowly and sat on the bed a few feet from her. She glanced at his lap, gawking a little at his hefty erection, and then jerked her gaze back up to his face when he spoke.

"What is insane about me helping you get past your fear of males?"

"I don't know you and you're naked."

He eased his hand toward her, palm out. "Take my hand."

She hesitated and then unlocked her fingers, actually putting her hand in his. He didn't comment on it if he noticed how she trembled. He inched her palm to his chest, placing it over his heart, and gently held it there. Heat radiated off his skin, more so than anyone she'd ever touched.

"You're very warm."

"You mentioned that before."

She had, believing he'd been sick with a fever. His hand released hers, leaving her touching him on her own. She gazed up into his beautiful eyes as her fingers inched up to his collarbone, hesitated there, and then slid upward to curve around the bend of his broad shoulder.

"There's no need to be timid. I will remain still," he encouraged her softly. "There's no pain here, Jill." He paused. "I will not harm you."

Honesty and sincerity shone in his eyes. Jill wanted to believe him but it would be insane to do so. She didn't know him—cyborgs had to be pretty dangerous, considering that Earth Government had tried to kill all of them—but her other hand lifted to touch his thigh inches above his knee. Hot skin greeted her there as well.

Coal took a shallow breath. "I'll lie down and you can explore me if you wish."

93

She released him and watched as he very slowly stretched out on the bed until he rested flat on his back. His arms rose and he laced his fingers behind his head, using his palms to form a pillow.

"Go ahead, Jill. You may explore any part of me you wish."

She turned to allow her gaze to travel over his impressive form. His beauty of his muscular, toned body wasn't lost on her. Even his unusual gray coloring attracted her, tempting her to spread her hands over him.

"Have you ever willingly touched a man?"

"No."

"What do you fear?"

Images of her past flashed. Her ex-husband had really hurt her and on top of it all, he'd been verbally abusive. She'd never wanted to touch a man before, never had been given the opportunity to do it without fear. It sank in slowly that she wasn't afraid. She felt curious, definitely, but memories of what Coal had done to her body had her feeling...aroused.

"I'm not sure," she admitted, caressing his thigh, amazed that the small amount of hair there could be so soft and that his warm skin could be silky textured, considering the strength of muscles lurking just beneath.

"There's no pain here," he assured her again. "I will never hurt you. I give my word on that."

Her gaze lifted up his body to meet his intense, beautiful eyes. Sincerity shone in those dark depths and she really wanted to believe him enough to put faith in his word.

"You can touch me anywhere, explore anything, and I will remain still."

Jill hesitated and then shifted on the bed, bending her knee, and turned to face him. Her other hand shook slightly when she reached over and firmly put her hand over his other thigh. She looked down, watching in amazement as his cock stiffened even more, rising straight up his belly.

"Go ahead," he urged. "Have you ever touched a male's sex?"

No. She bit her lower lip in nervousness when she concentrated on his stiff shaft. Her right hand slid up his thigh ever so slowly. When she nearly reached it, his cock moved, jerking slightly, and she froze.

"It's a normal reaction. I'm very turned on. Your hands are incredibly gentle and nearly torturing me with wanting more."

"You won't knock me over, pin me down, and force me to take you?"

His mouth tensed. "No. I really want five minutes alone with the male who put that terror into your eyes."

Her fear eased instantly and she smiled. "What would you do to the asshole?"

It was Coal's turn to hesitate. "I don't want to frighten you but I am capable of violence under certain circumstances. I'd love to hurt him the way he did you."

Her eyebrows shot up and her sense of humor kicked in. "You want to pin him down and force yourself on him?"

His eyes rounded with horror. "No! I am not into forcing sex on anyone and males do not turn me on. I would wish to terrify him and cause him pain."

She laughed, completely relaxing. "I was teasing."

"It isn't funny that a male harmed you."

Her smile died. "I know. Sometimes I deal with pain by making jokes. It's a defensive mechanism that's kept me sane when times turned really bad."

"I understand. Let's forget about the…" He paused. "Asshole."

Jill smiled again and lowered her attention to his cock. It surprised her how large he was, the darker gray color fascinating, and he had no hair there at all. Her hand moved, inching up until her fingertips brushed against the base of his shaft. He sucked in air but didn't ask her to stop. She glanced up, saw his eyes were closed now and then she openly studied the part of the male anatomy that she'd dreaded the most.

Her hand brushed the shaft tentatively at first. It stunned her that the skin there felt so smooth and velvety, though he had turned incredibly hard with desire. He took a deep breath, kept his eyes closed, and she grew bolder by attempting to encircle his cock. Her finger and thumb couldn't touch—his sex too thick for her to be able to do that.

She released him and braced a hand on the bed when she shifted her position until she hovered over his lap on her knees. The muscles that ran along his stomach up to his ribcage were tense, thick ridges under his skin. Her hand flattened there to feel them, intrigued by his physique.

"I've never seen anyone like you."

His dark eyes opened and met her gaze. "Cyborgs are different. I believe you'll adjust to my coloring."

"I meant how in shape you are. You're really strong, aren't you?"

His pink tongue darted out to swipe his lips while he watched her. "Yes. I'm noticeably stronger than human males."

Her gaze drifted down his body and then stopped at her hand resting on his belly. "Do you have metal parts inside?" She looked at his face, hoping the question wouldn't insult him.

"I have implants and some of my bones have been reinforced for hard labor."

A shiver went down her spine at the idea of what must have been done to him. "I'm sorry. Did it hurt?"

He shrugged. "We were created in laboratories and I was fully grown to adult male size by the time they allowed us to become conscious. They had finished producing me by that stage."

It sounded so cold and sterile to Jill. Sympathy for the big cyborg had her rubbing his skin again over his taunt belly, this time in hopes of soothing the sad look that sparked in his beautiful eyes.

"I'm sorry. Earth Government does a lot of horrible things since the wars ended and the countries became united. I think they let all that power get to the bureaucrats until they really do have a God complex."

"You aren't old enough to have been a part of what was done to me and I'm grateful to be alive." His face tensed, his lips pressing tightly together into a grim line. "My people are capable of hording power over the weaker class as well."

Jill hesitated to pry but she really wanted to know. Coal watched her too and then took a deep breath. His grim look made her wonder what had put that angry expression there.

"More male cyborgs were made than female ones. They had problems early on that made them halt production of our females."

"May I ask what that was?"

"Your males tried to use them for sex and when cyborg women fought back, they were killed. It wasn't cost effective to spend money to create something that wouldn't survive long enough to turn a profit."

Jill pulled her hand away from him and sat back on the bed, horrified. "Oh God."

Coal slowly sat up, careful not to startle her. "Cyborg females had difficult lives. There were very few of them compared to all the males and when we fled Earth their survival became our first priority."

"Did a lot of you escape?"

"I won't give you a number. I gave my word I'd free you and what you already know is far too much for Earth Government to learn."

"I wouldn't turn you in." It hurt a little that Coal thought she would but then, she reminded herself, they didn't know each other. "I swear."

"I refuse to give you numbers."

"Okay. It's not important but I hope a lot of you did." She meant it.

He watched her, studying her. His body relaxed after a few deep breaths. "I believe you."

"Good. I know we're different but you can trust me."

Coal slowly reached out to her. She tensed up but his hand just covered hers. Warm, gentle fingers curved around the back of her hand.

98

She noticed how much bigger his were compared to hers, dwarfing hers in his hold.

"Jill?"

Her gaze lifted. "Yes?"

He swallowed, his Adam's apple bobbing. "We're not so different and we have something in common."

She couldn't see it. They had drastically dissimilar pasts. She'd come from her mother's womb—he'd come from a laboratory. She had pink skin and he had gray. She didn't have reinforced bones, whatever that meant, but he did. They weren't similar in size by a long shot.

"We have both been used for sex against our will. I was forced to be a breeder to our females. I agreed to the tests and to attempt intercourse with a few females to discover if we were able to breed. I enjoyed the sex at first but when two of the females were impregnated I realized the gravity of the consequences."

"You have two kids?" For some reason she didn't like hearing that.

"I only willingly helped create two. The rest were a result of forced donations from my body."

Jill looked him over with a quick sweep. "You're telling me some of your own women really forced you to have sex?" She couldn't even imagine that. He had to be the biggest, strongest man she'd ever laid eyes on. She hadn't really believed him when he'd said it before, chalking it up to a plot to gain her trust, but she didn't think that way anymore. "You're so big."

"Our females are strong and I didn't wish to kill them when we fought. They would attack me in groups, restrain me, and give me drugs to confuse

99

my mind. When they ran out of drugs they operated to damage the implants in my head that allowed me to control my physical responses. They would torture me until my body complied. I could withhold any responses to the things they did to me until they damaged my implants."

Mute, Jill gaped at him.

"The implants allowed me to deaden parts of my body. We were created to work for humans and the physical labor could be very painful at times. They didn't want that to slow progression of our duties and the abilities to ignore any discomfort were deemed important. There were also risks of us being captured and they needed us to be impervious to pain if our captors attempted to torture company secrets from us. Of course we wouldn't have been as useful for some of the tasks they'd assigned us if they'd just stripped us of all our nerve endings. It also became a way to punish us. They could remotely activate and deactivate the chips as needed by our supervisors. They would shut off the chips to beat us as punishment and make us suffer the resulting pain for days until we healed."

Tears filled Jill's eyes, momentarily blinding her. "What the hell did they do to you?"

"The females or Earth Government?"

She'd always thought she'd gotten a raw deal in life with losing her mother so young, having to be raised by an aunt who kept her in seclusion from other people for her protection, and then learning what kind of man her father had been. Of course her years with her ex-husband had been a nightmare but he'd fed her, kept her clothed, and hadn't dared inflict much bodily harm except for the times he'd forced sex on her. Even then, while it hadn't been enjoyable in the least, he hadn't purposely caused her physical pain. He'd been more about terrifying her with threats to keep her under his control.

"Jill?"

"I'm just sorry you've had such a hard life."

He studied her. "It has made me stronger and more determined to survive."

She could relate to that. "The women..." She paused. "Did they really hurt you and humiliate you?"

He took a deep breath and then leaned in closer but didn't touch her. "It depended on which female had use of me. The worst thing they did to me was damage my implants and force the donation of my sperm. I am happy good came out of it from the flourish of children produced to advance our race but it saddens me that I wasn't permitted to know them. The females deemed me a slave and kept the children away from me at all times for fear that I might harm them. They feared I was capable of that since I didn't want to be used in that manner but I never would have done that. They are a part of me physically and therefore I would have done anything to protect the childre."

Questions filled her, so many she didn't know where to start. Coal spoke before she could ask any of them.

"I had to be secured flat on my back on a bed for them to torture as needed. They realized quickly that great bodily harm would make my body tense and cause adrenaline spikes that gave me erections. Earth Government had taught us how to inflict great pain while leaving no lasting physical damage. Once the pain became too much and they got the physical reaction they wanted, they would mount me until they got my seed. Every time they would come inside the room where they kept me I'd know hopelessness and dread of what would happen. Occasionally they had to allow me up to avoid sores forming where my skin never left the bed they kept me chained to. If I was lucky, occasionally they believed I had become less threatening and too weak to attack. I managed to escape a few times when they grew lax on the number of guards assigned to take me to the river."

He paused, watching Jill. She couldn't speak. The horror of what he said sank in.

"There were months when I'd be free until their hunting parties would find me again. When my brother cyborgs rescued us from the planet we'd crashed on and realized my circumstances, they freed me from the females. The females no longer have control over my body but they of course retained the children who were created by my sperm."

Jill didn't think, just reacted. She reached up and cupped his cheek, stared into his beautiful eyes, and blinked back tears that threatened to blind her. "I'm so sorry that happened to you."

His eyes widened in surprise and his hand lifted to her cheek to gently brush away a tear that slid down her face. When he spoke, he whispered, "You shed tears for me?"

She nodded. "Don't you ever cry?"

He pulled away from her touch and dropped his hand on the bed near her thigh. "A physical expression does not change the circumstances in my life or wash away the memories I must live with."

"Aren't you bitter?"

He shifted on the bed and looked away from her, shaking his head. "It would be a useless emotion that would only allow me to dwell on the wrongs committed against me. I wish to one day get past it and obtain a fulfilling life." He cleared his throat. "I must make the best of what has been done to me since there's no way to repair the damage to my implants."

His strength impressed her and it went far beyond his muscled body. "You're amazing."

He frowned and met her gaze again. "How so?"

She wasn't sure how to explain it to him. "You just are."

He gave her a perplexed look and she knew he didn't understand. She tried to find a way to express it to him. "When I got free of my ex-husband, I flat-out hated all men and swore them off. You've dealt with so much more and yet you haven't hurt or taken it out on me for what was done to you. You could. You have me at your mercy."

"You never harmed me, Jill. I'm in your debt and I'm willing to do this to repay you."

A horrible thought struck as her gaze flew down to his naked body. His erection had softened, his body reflecting his loss of interest in sex, and her mouth dropped open.

"Oh my God. I'm so sorry." She scrambled off the bed and grabbed a pillow as she got to her feet. She turned and pitched it at Coal, aiming for his lap.

His reflexes were lightning fast as he caught it and his body tensed. "You're attacking me with a pillow and apologizing for it?"

"No. Cover up. You did this for me, to pay me back, and you must hate me for putting you in this situation. You don't have to force yourself to touch me as a way to thank me." She spun, giving him her back. "I thought you were trying to get me to have sex with you but now I'm sure it's just traumatizing you. I'm so, so sorry!"

Chapter Six

Coal slowly rose to his feet and dropped the pillow on the bed. Jill stood in front of him, keeping her body turned away to give him privacy. The human had shocked him deeply with her perception of the situation they were in. She truly believed what she'd said, though she had come to the wrong conclusion.

"I don't hate you and I chose to fix you."

"You don't have to." She spoke so softly he barely caught her words. "Just put your pants on and don't do this to yourself. You've had enough women use your body for their own purposes and that's not why I saved you. I didn't expect anything for doing it. I just couldn't leave you there knowing what lay in store for you."

He took a step toward her and then another until he nearly touched her back. Desire heated his blood when he noticed just how much of her legs were exposed in her shirt. If she lifted her arms it would rise to expose the bottom of her ass. His cock hardened and his hands twitched to touch her.

"I want to fix you but that isn't the only reason I decided to show you pleasure is possible between males and females."

Jill turned her head to stare up at him over her shoulder. Their gazes met and held for long moments. She had an expressive face and he liked that. The more time he spent with her the better he learned to read her. Right at that moment he knew she didn't quite believe him.

"I'm very attracted to you and curious if mutual sexual relations between us would be pleasurable. I've had these thoughts since you cleaned the oatmeal from my body."

"Really?" The tense lines around her mouth eased.

Coal bit back a groan. If he knew it wouldn't frighten her, he'd show her how much he wanted her. He'd never ached to have a woman before without drugs or extreme forced stimulation. Jill just standing near him had him wishing he could toss her on the bed and take her. The memory of the taste of her arousal, the sounds she made as he'd licked her, had blood filling his cock until it hurt—turning steel hard. He would never forget how soft, wet, and tight she'd been when he'd finger-fucked her.

"Take your shirt off and return to the bed." He hoped she'd do it.

Jill turned to face him and her shirt brushed his protruding sex. He held still as she looked down at his cock. She backed away quickly as she gasped in obvious surprise at what she'd touched. He gripped her arms to keep her from tripping. They both froze.

"We'll help each other get beyond our past experiences."

Her hesitation made him regret what he'd told her.

"I—"

"I made a mistake by sharing too much of my past with you," he admitted, stopping her from telling him no. "I believed it would put you at ease but instead I've given you the impression that sex between us would traumatize me. That's what you stated. That isn't factual. I want you."

* * * * *

106

Jill took a deep breath and blew it out, not looking away as he watched her so intently. "I'm glad you told me everything."

"I'm not, if you refuse to allow me to touch you."

She couldn't resist looking down at his hard-on. He definitely had to be interested in sex. She stared at the proof. The warm hands gently gripping her upper arms let go and he backed up to the bed. She held still and just watched him sit on the edge of the mattress, spread his thighs, and then he ease back to rest his weight on his elbows.

"Come to me."

His commanding tone called to her for some reason as she gawked at his perfect body stretched out fully, naked on her bed. The picture he made had her body responding to his strong sexual appeal.

"This is nuts."

Coal smiled. "You enjoyed what I did to you with my mouth. Allow me to do it again. I want to. I take pleasure from it as well."

Her nipples tingled and her belly quivered in response. She took another step and then another until she paused near his legs. "Okay."

He turned on his side and patted the bed next to him. "Stretch out here."

Temptation and a rush of desire enticed Jill. She touched her shirt, considering taking it off, but then shyness gripped her. She got on the bed, her leg brushing his when she rolled over onto her back. Coal turned more on his side and she settled flat. Her heart pounded hard.

"I don't know what to do," she admitted to him.

The color of his eyes darkened with desire. "I do. Just relax and allow me to touch you. Trust me not to hurt you."

Staring into those incredible eyes of his she wanted desperately to believe him. Her body relaxed and she gave him a sharp nod. "Okay."

He lifted up and slid off the bed. She raised her head to watch him when he reached for something on the floor and didn't say a word when he removed the vent seal from the pocket of his discarded pants. Her arms slid on her sheets when she used them to push her chest up to get a better look at the lower half of Coal's body. In stunned silence she watched him stretch the band and put it on.

"Doesn't that hurt?"

"No. It's not too tight."

She had to take his word for it but she couldn't see how it wouldn't. She lay flat again, thinking it better not to stare at his cock any more or the green band he'd just fit snuggly at the base of his shaft. Instead she tried to relax and not lose her nerve. Coal wanted to repeat what he'd done to her before, only this time she wasn't tied down. Her fingers clutched at the bedding just for something to cling to.

Strong hands gently gripped her knees and Jill jumped slightly at his touch. Coal's hold remained loose and he gave her a tense smile.

"Easy. Just relax. Close your eyes if that will help and just allow me to adjust you."

She nodded, squeezing her eyes closed, and took a deep breath. She relaxed again and didn't tense up when Coal's hold tightened to spread her knees far apart. Her cheeks warmed, knowing he could see every part of her sex when he pulled her closer to the edge of the bed, parting her thighs wider.

"You have no idea how beautiful I think you are."

The deep tone of his voice had her nipples hardening and excitement raced through her when his warm breath fanned her inner thighs.

"If you knew how eager I am to do this, you'd never question how much I want to touch and taste you."

Jill's breathing increased as her heart beat faster in anticipation. The memory of what he'd done to her had her feeling a little eager herself. She tensed a bit when his thumbs spread her sex lips apart and his tongue lightly touched her clit. She made a small sound in the back of her throat when he hesitated and then licked the small bud.

A moan broke from her parted lips. Pleasure had her nails digging into her mattress where she clutched the sheets. She spread her thighs wider on her own to give him better access. Coal groaned against her sensitive flesh and the pace increased along with the pressure he applied.

"Oh God," she moaned. "It feels so good it almost hurts." She wiggled in his hold, breaking the connection between her body and his mouth.

Coal's mouth left her and Jill's opened her eyes to stare down at him. Their gazes locked but he didn't speak. Instead he changed his hold on her legs, wrapping his big arms around them from the underside, lifting her lower body higher until the back of her thighs rested on his biceps. He reached over her, pinning her legs between his arms, and then spread her apart again with his hands. He looked away from her to stare at her pussy a second before he dipped his head, mouth parting.

109

Jill arched her back, eyes closing again when she realized what he'd done. She couldn't move her hips now. He had her thighs pinned open but his strength didn't frighten her. His lips closed around her clit and he began to suckle her with strong tugs that had her crying out in ecstasy while the flat of his tongue rubbed furiously up and down on her throbbing bud. Pleasure turned into nearly raw pain and when she became certain she would die from it, the climax tore through her. Jill cried out, her body shaking from the intensity of it.

She realized his hold on her legs eased and she didn't even wonder what he'd do next when he released her legs and put her feet flat on the mattress. Her thighs remained open but she didn't have the strength to close them. The bed dipped near the end as more weight came down on it. Hot skin brushed her inner thighs and then against her arm where it rested over her head. Weight eased down on top of her, pinning her flat, and that made her open her eyes.

Coal hovered over her, his body barely touching hers, and his beautiful dark eyes looked nearly black as their gazes held. He'd braced his arms next to her chest. His skin looked darker to her and passion hardened his features until he nearly looked grim but she understood.

"I want you. Please say yes. I'll be gentle."

He wanted inside her body. The image of his large cock was fused into her brain. Coal wasn't making her take him though, he had asked, and she knew he wasn't her ex-husband. He not only didn't look anything similar to the asshole she'd married but Coal had shown her that sex could be amazing, intensely pleasurable, and she wanted to know if he'd feel good

110

inside her. He also faced her, something her ex had never done, always taking her from behind after he'd pinned her.

"I'm a little afraid but we can try it."

His eyes closed and she nearly laughed at the obvious relief he didn't even bother to hide. She smiled instead and some of her fear eased. This wasn't Darren. This was Coal, the cyborg who'd never hurt her, who'd had dozens of chances to harm her but hadn't. She released the bedding, watching him take deep breaths, and her hands trembled a little when she touched his chest, hovering over hers.

His eyes snapped open when her fingers brushed his warm skin and she froze, unsure if she was allowed to trace his skin. A soft groan came from Coal and he licked his lips, his attention fixing on her mouth.

"I want to kiss you."

Jill licked her lips to wet them and her hands slid up to his neck. He wasn't pulling away from her touch so it encouraged her to continue her exploration. She traced both sides of his neck and then her hands cupped his strong cheekbones.

"You can."

Coal lowered his mouth and Jill closed her eyes, raising her head a little to meet him. She wasn't sure what to expect but the brush of incredibly soft lips wasn't it. Coal had a hard-looking mouth but his gentleness shouldn't have surprised her. Coal looked scary as hell with his cyborg size and distinctions but appearances were deceiving when it came to the incredibly sweet cyborg.

111

He deepened the kiss, his tongue delving into her welcoming mouth. It shocked her a little when she tasted herself on him, having momentarily forgotten what he'd just done to her, but it only turned her on more. The gentle kisses turned more aggressive but she met his passion easily and her hands left his face to wrap around his neck. An ache started again and she arched her back to press her breasts against Coal's chest.

Frustration flared when she realized she couldn't feel his hot skin as well with her shirt on. She broke the kiss and stared into Coal's black eyes. They really did change colors, she realized, when passion gripped him.

"Do you want me to stop?" His voice had grown so deep he nearly snarled the words but no anger showed in his features. Instead he looked concerned. "I will go slower."

"I want the shirt off. I want to feel us touching," she admitted.

Coal pushed up, braced his entire weight with one hand, and his other hand gripped the front of her shirt. To her shock, he tore it open. Material just shredded from his strength and revealed her breasts and stomach when it parted.

"Sorry." Coal froze. "I'm scaring you, aren't I?" He tossed away the destroyed material. "I didn't mean to do that."

She forced her lungs to work. "It's okay."

Her hands shook as she maneuvered under him. He kept his upper chest lifted away from hers while she worked the rest of the shirt out from under her back and pushed it away from them. She settled flat and met his gaze again, seeing regret on his features. She concentrated on that instead

112

of acknowledging that she lay under Coal, completely naked now. She didn't want to feel embarrassed or self-conscious about her nudity.

"I'm very turned on and I wanted to give you what you wanted. I should have gently removed it from you instead of just ripping it off."

She suddenly laughed, the humor of the situation hitting her. "I'm okay. It startled me but you didn't terrify me or anything. I hated that shirt anyway."

"Are you sure?" He studied her eyes. "If you want to stop we can."

That settled it for Jill. "I don't want to stop." She nearly laughed again but refrained from the obvious relief that flashed on Coal's face. "I want to know it all."

Coal slowly lowered his chest until they were skin to skin. The feeling of his hot flesh pressed to hers did things to Jill. Wonderful sensations flooded her body and her hands gripped his shoulders.

"I trust you," she admitted softly. "I'm a little afraid it's going to hurt because it always has but I've never wanted anyone before either. The only man I've ever known never made me ache the way you do. There's no comparison but I just wanted you to know."

"I've never wanted anyone the way I do you," Coal admitted. "I'll kill myself before I cause you pain."

"Kiss me and let's do this. I really want to."

Coal hesitated. "I want this to be really good for you. I realize most humans prefer sex in this position but would you allow me to take you another way?"

Jill frowned. "What other way?"

"Do you trust me?"

She nodded. "Yeah. You haven't hurt me and I believe you won't."

He lowered his head and planted a kiss on her that left her panting for more. His lips left hers and he pushed up. Jill wanted to protest as she watched him sit on his bent legs between hers. In the next instant she gasped when he gripped her hips and lifted her until her ass rested on the top of his thighs. His cock ended up trapped between his thighs and under her ass.

Jill's eyes widened and alarm slammed her. "Not there!"

"I'm not going to do what you're thinking. I'm just going to prepare you for sex and need closer access to you. We're not going to attempt anal sex so relax. Reach up and brace your hands on something."

"What are you going to do?"

Coal smiled tensely. "Making sure I don't hurt you and that you're so into the sex that you welcome me entering you. I know what I'm doing."

"Okay." Jill nodded and reached up to grab handfuls of sheet. "I'm ready."

His smile reached his eyes. "You look as though you're preparing for something painful. This won't hurt."

"Right. Have you seen the size of your dick?"

He chuckled. "Here we go."

Coal spread her thighs wider apart on his lap and his thumb rubbed her clit. That wasn't what Jill expected him to do. He didn't try to enter her at all but instead tormented her by tracing circles on her oversensitive sex.

She spread her legs wider apart, moaning, and wiggled as the pleasure built.

Jill realized when Coal spread his thighs and allowed her ass to slip down into the cradle of his bent legs a little but she was too wrapped up in the wonderful feeling of his thumb teasing her clit. He purposely kept her from coming when her body began to tense for pending release. She bucked her hips in frustration.

"Please," she pleaded.

"Jill? Look at me."

Her eyes opened and she met his gaze.

He lifted his hips a little and her eyes widened when something large and hard pressed against her very wet pussy. His thumb pressed tighter on her clit and she moaned loudly, her eyes nearly closing from the pleasure but she fought not to look away from Coal. He pushed against her, his cock breaching her very slow, and the delightful sensation of being filled and stretched nearly overwhelmed her.

Coal got a pained expression and he groaned deeply. His thumb rubbed faster on her clit as he filled her, making her take inches more of his cock. He paused and then withdrew a little before pushed back in, allowing her to adjust to being fucked.

Raw bliss gripped Jill. Her hands released the sheets and she grabbed Coal's thighs next to her ass, clutching him in a death grip. He froze, not moving at all.

"Am I hurting you?"

She shook her head, unable to speak, panting instead. She bucked her hips, feeling him move inside her, and moaned in response. She repeated that wonderful movement that felt unbelievably good and moaned louder, encouraging him to continue.

"Jill," Coal rasped. "I'm losing it."

He moved and Jill threw her head back, crying out in ecstasy as Coal fucked her harder. His powerful hips stimulated them both, rocking his cock into her faster, going deeper with each motion, while his thumb strummed her clit. He felt incredibly rigid as he stretched her, awaking a fire inside Jill that threatened to burn her alive, and then she screamed out as she came so hard she wondered if she'd die from a heart attack.

Coal drove into her and then roared out over her dying scream. His hips jerked, his body shook violently, and Jill opened her eyes as she felt warmth spreading deep inside her pussy where he remained connected to her. She stared up at the most beautiful sight she'd ever seen.

Coal's head was thrown back, his mouth parted, and a look of pure sated passion softened his quickly relaxing features. The sheen of sweat on his chest and arms did funny things to her stomach and had her vaginal muscles gripping and caressing Coal's cock inside her or it may have just been them still twitching from the aftermath of the amazing sex they'd just had. A smile curved his lips and his chin lowered until he opened those sexy eyes of his to stare into hers.

"Please tell me I didn't hurt you."

Jill's heart did a funny thing in her chest and she blinked back tears that filled them instantly. Coal's smile faded and he slowly leaned down, his body curving around hers, and she swore she saw regret in his look. It about killed her to see it since that's the last thing she wanted him to feel.

"You didn't hurt me."

"Then why are you crying? I was too rough, wasn't I? You're very tight and smaller than I am."

Her hands lifted to cup his face to pull it closer to hers. "It's just that it was so amazing and your first concern is me."

"This makes you cry?"

She smiled at his confused look. "Yeah. It does. You're amazing, Coal. I've never met anyone as wonderful as you. You really care if I enjoyed that and trust me, I did."

"I lost my control," he admitted. One of his hands curved around her hip, holding her on his lap while his other hand gently brushed a lock of her hair away from her cheek. "Are you certain I wasn't too rough?"

Jill nodded. "That was just perfect. I never knew it could be this way."

His smile returned. "That was just one position. There are a lot more of them that may feel even better to you."

"Are we going to try them?" *Please say yes*, Jill thought.

"Do you want to?"

She nodded, knowing she blushed.

His fingers caressed her cheek and then to her regret, he slowly withdrew from her body as his still-hard cock eased from her pussy. She'd enjoyed feeling fused to him.

"I don't want to make you sore since you're not used to sex. We'll try another position in a few hours. Go ahead and use the cleansing unit. I need to check your quarters for weapons and then perhaps you can help me with some of the repairs I plan to make. It would be helpful if I taught you how to do certain things."

"Sure."

Jill hated when he left her, climbing from the bed, and no longer touching her. She grabbed the sheet and wrapped it around her body. It stung a little that he still wanted to make sure she wasn't stashing weapons in her room. It also didn't sit well with her that he had no plans to share a cleansing unit with her. Even her ex-bastard had hauled her into one with him after sex but of course that had been because he never trusted she wouldn't attack him in a vulnerable situation.

Coal removed the vent-seal cock ring, tossed it into her trash, and pulled up his pants. "I estimate it will take you five minutes to use the facilities and another five to get dressed. I'll be done with my search by then. When you come out, I'll be down the hall getting clean and changing my clothing. I'll return for you soon." He paused, his gaze lingering on the sheet hiding her body. "Go on."

Jill kept hold of the sheet as she scooted off the bed. She refused to walk naked across the room even if they'd just had sex together. Coal watched her without comment, allowing her to close the door between them. She leaned against the door and let her head hang.

She was afraid she'd get used to him or worse, maybe even fall for him. He was just too damn sexy and sweet. "Sucker tattooed in big block letters right across my ass," she muttered.

"What did you say, Jill? I didn't hear you."

She mouthed a silent curse, forgetting he'd planned to stick around her room for a few minutes to search it. "I was just muttering to myself."

He said nothing. She rolled her eyes, pushing away from the door, and headed for the cleanser. *Now he probably thinks I'm nuts for talking to myself*, she thought. *Just great!*

Chapter Seven

"Hand me the white pen tool."

Jill grinned and handed it over to Coal. "What is it really called?" He'd learned fast that using the technical names for tools had been a useless endeavor.

A smile flashed as he turned his head to stare at her. "It is a fusion applicator. I am going to fix Arm's damaged finger and return movement of it to him."

"Huh." Jill glanced at the shutdown droid. "I didn't know there was anything wrong with it."

"It's the smallest one and not used much but I noticed it while studying his hands when he held me in the cargo hold."

"I'm sorry about that. I didn't want to keep you locked down but you terrified me."

Coal reached over and brushed his fingers across her thigh. "I understand and you were being reasonable to assume I would be dangerous." His hand left her to accept the tool. He turned and bent over Arm's hand, working silently.

Jill stared at Coal's broad back and couldn't help but notice the way muscles moved as his arms did. Her throat turned dry and she swallowed hard. She realized her body reacted when just looking at him and memories of what they'd done in her bed surfaced quickly. Her nipples hardened under the shirt she wore and it came as a shock when an ache started between her thighs.

"Hand me the red and green metal tool that resembles a hook," he stated softly.

Jill didn't move. Instead she continued to stare at him until his head turned, drawing her attention away from his broad back.

"Jill? Are you all right? You look a little flushed."

"Uh, yeah."

He turned to face her. "What is wrong?"

"I…" She wasn't sure what to say, not wanting to admit that she wished he'd put down the tools and touch her instead.

"Are you hungry?"

"No."

"What is wrong? Are you tired?"

"Seeing you without your shirt does things to me." She felt proud that she'd managed to blurt it out.

A small smile played at his lips. "What kind of things?"

"I want to touch you."

The smile died and Coal put down the tool. He swiveled in the chair to face her and leaned back, his hands brushing the top of his thighs. "Come here."

Temptation could be a terrible thing when one wasn't sure what to do. Jill hesitated and then stood to move closer. Coal reached for her and used her hips to guide her until she straddled his lap. It made them nearly eye level with Coal only a few inches taller. His hands remained on her.

"Go ahead."

Her hands didn't tremble when she placed her palms flat on his chest. His hot skin and his masculine scent had her on sensory overload. The intense reaction of her body from looking at him made her lean in closer, wishing she had the courage to kiss him.

"You may touch me any time you wish, Jill."

"You don't mind?"

He shook his head. "I would strongly encourage it. Are you sore at all?" He glanced down where her legs were spread far apart across his thighs.

"I'm achy but it's not from being tender."

His chest quickly expanded with his quick intake of air then he met her gaze. "You want me."

"I've never experienced anything as wonderful as what we shared." She decided to be totally honest. "You're going to be gone soon and I want to feel that way again."

Coal's expression softened and he slowly grinned. "I've helped you get past your aversion to males."

"No."

Dark eyebrows arched and the smile faded. "You don't want to have sex with me?"

"I don't want anything to do with other men." She chose her words carefully. "I do want you though."

The hands on her hips gripped her tightly. "I am a man, Jill." Anger deepened his voice. "I'm not one of your androids."

"I know that. I didn't mean—"

"I am a sentient being with desires, needs, and emotions," he growled.

"I'm not saying you aren't." She inwardly winced, knowing she'd messed this up somehow. "I just meant that you're the only man I want to touch."

Some of his anger eased from his features and his hold loosened. "I believe I understand."

"Good." Jill tried to get up. "I should let you get back to work."

"No." Coal refused to release her. "Touch me and allow me to touch you."

She hesitated. "Would you kiss me?"

He didn't hesitate and Jill closed her eyes an instant before his mouth found hers. He didn't go for a soft, timid kiss. Coal's mouth came down hard and demanding. He forced his tongue between her parted lips, sliding in and tasting every part of her he could reach. She moaned and her arms wrapped around his neck until her chest pressed tightly against his.

Her body lifted when he slid down some in the chair until his ass was at the edge of the seat. Strong hands pulled her forward, higher up his body until she moaned when the ridge of his aroused cock, trapped in his pants, rubbed against her clit where his thighs had her legs spread wide apart. Even through their clothing the pleasure became intense.

Her rocked against her, the friction of their bodies sending sheer delight coursing through her. His hold on her shifted when he released her hips. One of his arms hooked around her at the back of her ass, pulling her even tighter against his cock. She registered the tug on her shirt then his hand slid against her ribs. His big, hot hand cupped one of her bare breasts and sent even more raw sensations to her brain. She couldn't believe how incredible he could make her feel, though their pants were still on.

Coal swallowed her ragged moans with his hot, passionate kiss. His tongue dominated her mouth as easily as he used his strong arm to help her ride his thrusting hips as his cock rubbed against her clit. Her nails dug into his shoulders when she thought she couldn't take the ecstasy swamping her. When his finger and thumb pinched her erect nipple it became the last shot of rapture that sent her into climax. She cried out against his tongue.

A snarl came from Coal when he tore his mouth from hers. They both panted and then before the tremors of release could subside, his body stopped moving. Trembling, Jill opened her eyes to stare into his, now black with passion. He tore her shirt near the hem when he freed his hand from beneath it and he gripped her hips again.

She gasped, still clinging to him when he lifted her to place her on her shaking knees on the deck between his spread thighs. She collapsed to sit on her heels unable to hold her body up. He pushed the chair back and shot to his feet. His hands gripped the waist of his pants. He just tore them open down the front seam instead of unfastening them to free his very-swollen cock.

"Take off your pants," he ordered in a deep, ragged voice. "I have to have you."

Jill stared up at Coal and licked her lips. She'd come but he hadn't. He wanted her so badly she could see him fighting not to lunge at her, his body trembling with need the way hers did from the aftermath of her climax.

"Please, Jill." His desperate gaze locked with hers. "I'm so close I won't last long but I want inside you." He remained frozen where he stood, waiting for her to respond. "I'll be gentle but I hurt to have you."

Her clit throbbed, sensitive from the harsh rubbing of material against it, and her inner vaginal walls still twitched from coming. She licked her lips. His cock twitched, so incredibly hard he stood straight out. It took her a second but she pulled her strength together and rose up to her knees.

"Sit down."

He blinked, a confused look crossed his features, but then he nodded. "You want on top to mount me."

She watched him shove his destroyed pants down to his knees and he just dropped back into the chair. His weight made the chair groan but it didn't break. She walked on her knees forward and then reached for him with her hands. The second her fingertips brushed the shaft of his cock he let out a loud groan.

"Don't tease me, honey. I'm really close. I don't have much control right now."

That drew a smile from her as she glanced up at his very serious expression. His cock twitched again, pulling away from her hesitant touch, and then returned. Jill drew her tongue over her lips to wet them, her full attention lowering back to his lap. She'd always wondered what it would be like but never had any desire to really find out until that moment. She inched closer, her hand wrapping firmly around the lower section of his shaft.

"I've never done this before but I've read about it in my fiction files."

"You just remove your pants and just sit on my lap the way you were. I'll ease you down carefully so you can adjust to me. We'll go slowly."

She pushed back her hair with her free hand and then moved before he could tell her no. Her mouth opened and she bent her head, hovering over his cock. She heard him gasp but she didn't look away from the tip of his cock under her parted lips. Her tongue slid out and she hesitantly ran it over the velvety crown.

Something creaked loudly but Coal didn't move or protest. She released her hair and gripped the top of his bare thigh to keep her balance. A taste teased her tongue and she hesitated, closing her mouth then running his cock head along the roof of her mouth. He tasted sweet. It surprised her and she liked the taste. Her mouth parted again and her hold on his cock tightened slightly to keep him still. She ran her tongue again over the tip of him, more sweetness coming from the crown of his cock, from the slight wetness she found there at the slit.

A deep groan came from Coal but he still didn't move his hips at all or order her to stop. The muscles under her hand tensed though. She grew braver and took a few inches of his cock inside her mouth. She avoided scraping it with her teeth, though he was so thick that she had to really open up to allow him in. She sealed her lips around his girth and sucked slowly, getting a feel for how to do it.

* * * * *

Coal threw his head back, his heart threatening to explode from how hard it beat against his ribs. His hand still gripped the part of the chair he'd accidentally snapped off from the underside of when Jill had licked him. The sensation of her heated, wet mouth tentatively sucking a few inches of his cock had to be the worst but most wonderfully pleasurable torture he'd ever experienced.

She moaned and it sent vibrations gently down his shaft to his tight balls. He fought hard not to come right there. Sweat beaded his brow while he concentrated on his breathing, trying to slow it to get any control at all over his body. She moved her head, taking a little more of his shaft into her mouth. When she pulled up, the slide of her tongue along the underside of his cock made him clench his teeth.

Don't come, he ordered his body. *Hang on. If you release, you'll startle her and she'll stop.* His body seemed not to want that so some of the pain in his balls eased but just slightly. His eyes were squeezed tightly closed while he hoped his teeth wouldn't break as he bit down harder when Jill started to move up and down on him. Rapture at what she could do to him became his sole focus. Her hand gripping his shaft moved, pumping him in tune to what her phenomenal mouth did to him.

"I'm coming," he groaned, unable to hold back any longer.

She didn't jerk away or stop. Instead she sucked harder, moving faster, taking even more of him. He roared out and threw the broken piece of chair away, freeing his hand to frantically grab the underside of the chair with both of them to lock his ass to it so he didn't thrust up into her throat, terrified he'd choke her if he forced her to take more of him. Fear over scaring her and extreme bliss blurred together when his cock pulsed.

She swallowed when he filled her mouth with his cum. The ecstasy at the added sensation had him crying out again. His tense body shook and when it ended after she released him gently with her mouth, he turned completely limp. He panted, eyes still closed, and his head fell forward. A deep sense of utter paradise settled throughout him.

"I take it I did that right?" Jill's hesitant voice broke him from his euphoria.

Coal lifted his head, opened his eyes, and gazed at her with pure adoration. He couldn't stop the smile that curved his lips. She had to be the most beautiful woman he'd ever seen. Her mouth looked redder than normal, a little swollen, and a slight pinkness spread across her cheeks. *Absolutely adorable*, he thought, realizing how shy she looked and how unsure of her sexual skills.

His body didn't want to move yet but he forced it to. He held out his hands to her. "Come here."

He took note of the way her hands trembled a little when she placed them in his palms and how delicate they were in comparison to his own. She seemed so fragile—humans were—and he tugged her closer. She came, moving between his spread thighs again, and he lifted one of her hands, turned it over, and brought it to his mouth. He pressed a kiss to her soft palm. He saw her stunned look. "Thank you."

Her eyebrows shot up and she blushed more. "You've gone down on me and I wanted to try it with you."

"Did you get pleasure from it?" He hoped so because he really wanted her to do that again in the near future.

"You taste good and…" She bit her lip, something he had noted that she did often when nervousness came into play. "I did."

His grin widened until the muscles in his face protested. "I've never had a female do that to me before and you nearly killed me from how wonderful it felt."

Shock blanked her features and his smile died.

"Should I have not admitted that to you?" Uncertainty gripped him, not wanting her to react negatively. He wasn't similar to other males, his life had made him different, and he hoped she wouldn't pity him for something she obviously considered odd about him.

"Nobody ever gave you head?" Her astonishment couldn't be clearer.

He shook his head, keeping hold of her hands. "No."

"But didn't any of those women ever try that to turn you on?"

"It was never about my pleasure but theirs. They used pain to stimulate my body."

Jill jerked her hands out of his and he inwardly winced. He needed to stop informing her about what had, or in this case, hadn't been done to him. She suddenly lunged at him. He tensed, stunned she'd attack him, but her arms slid around him instead, wrapping around his neck tightly in a hug. Her body pressed firmly against his chest. She turned her head until her lips brushed his throat.

"I'm so sorry for what those bitches did to you, Coal. Any time you want me to do that to you again, just tell me."

129

A sense of happiness flooded him, nearly blinding him as his eyes watered and his arms wrapped around her to draw her up his body until he had her across his lap. He held her and she seemed willing to allow it when her arms continued to cling to him.

"Thank you, Jill."

"How about if I send Arm after those women? He can kick some serious ass."

The unexpected laugh poured from his chest. "Arm?"

She nodded against his throat. "Yeah. Can you imagine their faces when he came at them full speed to get some revenge for you? You should have seen your face when you first saw him. Someone should kick their sorry asses for what they did to you. I'd do it myself but I'm not really a fighter." She paused. "I wouldn't order him to kill them but I'd sure like to tell him to break some arms and legs."

Coal hated to do it but he released her enough to pull back to study her upturned face. "Don't even joke about it. I never want my people to have a reason to see you as the enemy. There are far more of them than you'd suspect. I appreciate the sentiment though. They can no longer harm me. I'm free."

"It just makes me really mad."

"I understand. I would love five minutes in a room with your asshole."

The laugh she gave him astonished him, not sure what he'd said in such a serious moment that she'd found humorous. Perhaps the idea of him harming her ex-husband made her that joyously happy. He'd sincerely hunt that human down if it pleased Jill and removed some of the sadness caused to her.

"I thought you said we weren't going to have anal sex." The teasing look glinting in her beautiful blue eyes demonstrated that she'd understood his context but had chosen to joke about it.

He grinned. "Your sense of humor is growing on me."

"Good." She winked. "I'm not having anal sex with you though." Her grin faded. "You're way too big."

He laughed. "I can easily accept that."

The chair suddenly made a crunching noise and Coal tensed as it collapsed under them. His hold on Jill shifted, protectively trying to shield her from harm with his arms when they hit the floor hard. She landed on top of him.

Jill gaped at the broken pieces next to them.

"Are you harmed?" His first concern was to make certain she hadn't gotten hurt.

She shook her head. "You?"

He didn't mention that a piece of metal dug uncomfortably against his bare ass cheek but he didn't feel any pain, assessing that the skin hadn't broken. The seat had remained under him for the most part while the legs and back of it had scattered in a debris pattern around them. "I'm fine."

Jill laughed. "I guess we were too heavy for it."

Coal looked toward the piece of the chair he'd snapped off earlier and tossed away. He didn't want to admit he'd probably damaged it, made the seat unstable, in order to avoid digging his fingers into Jill's lovely red hair when she'd wrapped her mouth around his cock.

"That's more than logical," he said in a serious tone.

Jill planted a quick kiss on his cheek and then wiggled on his lap. "We should find you some pants and clean up this mess."

He hated to let her go but he did, helping her rise to her feet. "Good plan."

What he really wanted though would be to sweep her into his arms, carry her to her quarters, and remove the rest of her clothing. He could happily spend days, weeks, even months pleasuring Jill.

Chapter Eight

Jill grinned, watching Coal toss the pieces of chair into the trash recycler while she put away the tools. The pants he'd changed into were too tight, revealing a nice ass when they stretched to the point of the seams possibly bursting, and made her wish they would, just to see him bare again. A warm sensation surged inside her chest so strongly it had her heart racing. Her happiness faded to be replaced quickly with sobering realization.

"Oh hell."

Coal turned, his beautiful eyes meeting hers. "What is wrong?"

A lump formed in her throat and she had to swallow it down. "Nothing."

A dark eyebrow lifted. "Jill?"

"I just remembered I don't have another mobile chair in here," she lied. *I'm falling in love with him*, she thought. *Deeply.*

"I'm sorry I'm not able to fix it."

"It's fine." She forced a smile. "No worries. I'll pick up another one the next time I go to a dump planet. That's where I got that one. I probably should have left it there considering it obviously wasn't well made."

He gave her a sharp nod, turned away, and continued to clean up pieces. Jill spun to give him her back in case he glanced her way. She closed her eyes tightly and took a deep breath.

Don't do this, she ordered silently. *He's a person, he wants to go back to his cyborg people, and you can't keep him the way you did the droids.*

"I believe that's the last of it."

She opened her eyes and turned, forcing another smile. "Hungry? I am."

He nodded. "I could eat."

"Good. I have canned roast beef I've been saving for a special occasion. Have you ever had it? It's not simulated meat. It's the real stuff, straight from Earth."

"I haven't, but I trust it will be delicious if it's a special treat you have hoarded."

She laughed. "Hoarded?"

"Saved?" He grinned. "Is that better?"

"Yes. I also have some—"

"Incoming traffic," Fray announced over the speakers. "Two vessels."

Fear gripped Jill. Coal's features tensed.

"Follow me."

He spun quickly and strode toward the cargo hold doors. Jill remained still for a split second and then compelled her body into action, jogging after him. He kept a steady, fast pace and she had to upgrade to a run to keep up with him.

"Move," Coal demanded the second he entered the piloting station.

Fray abandoned his seat quickly and moved to the wall to keep out of the way. Jill had to catch her breath as she hovered just inside the doorway, watching Coal sink into the pilot seat to stare at the readings.

"It's not the freighter we attacked," he informed her. "They are coming into range from the direction we are traveling." He paused. "Come here, Jill."

She pushed forward and came around the chair to his side. One glance at the screen showed her two blinking lights and as she watched, they moved closer to the *Jenny*, heading right for them.

"Open communications and demand to know who they are and why they are approaching." Coal turned his head to stare up at her. "Can I trust you not to send them a distress message that you need help?"

It hurt that he still didn't trust her but she pushed it back, her fear stronger than the pain in her chest. "I wouldn't do that to you."

"Your system is so outdated I can't get a lock on what classifications they are. I hope they aren't Earth Government battle cruisers."

"Me too," she muttered. "I'm probably wanted by them, remember?" She hesitated. "If they are and they decide to board us I want you to hide. There's a false bottom under my bed where some illegal shit had once been stored. I found it by accident. They'll never find you unless they bring scanners aboard. This shuttle is too old for them to bother to confiscate and they will just arrest me, leaving the ship abandoned to float in space. That's what they do when they arrest people. Once they take me away you fly out of here but wait until they are out of range before you start the engines. I'm sure they will leave the droids behind with you." She paused.

"All I ask of you is to please take care of them for me. I don't want them ending up in a trash pile somewhere or aimlessly drifting in space aboard an abandoned ship."

His jaw clenched. "Hail them."

She nodded and reached over his arm to turn on the coms system then, before she spoke, she flipped another switch that made Coal frown. "This is the captain of the *Jenny*. I'm hailing the two inbound vessels approaching. Why are you tracking our ship?"

Coal turned off the com. "What is that?" He pointed to the extra switch.

"It's a voice modifier. I took saved messages from my father to this ship that the computer had stored when he communicated to the old crew and it's his voice that is being broadcast right now instead of mine. I use it to fool people I trade with to make them think he's talking to me instead of one of my droids when they check in on me while I'm off the shuttle. I also use it when dealing with unknown ships. It would be stupid to let them hear a woman's voice this far out. I may as well send out a signal telling them to attack me." She could see that he was uncertain. Jill reached out and squeezed his biceps, her fingers rubbing his hot skin. "Trust me."

Coal relaxed and flipped the com system back on. He gave her a grim nod.

"I'm speaking to the two inbound ships. Identify and state why you are tracking my ship."

A crackle sounded from the speakers. "This is the commander of the *Star*. We're searching for a life pod that accidently launched during a training exercise." Silence ticked. "There is a reward if you've picked it up or seen it on your long-range radar."

Coal hunched forward. "Who is speaking?"

Another hesitation. "My name is Flint. Have you seen the pod or know of its location?"

Coal suddenly leaned back and a grin spread across his face. To Jill's shock, he flicked off the voice modifier. He looked up at her and winked.

"Not only have I seen it, Flint..." he chuckled, "it was a tight fit. I don't recommend traveling in one."

Jill's knees wanted to collapse under her when it dawned on what he'd said. He looked away from her as the other man responded.

"Coal? Is that you?"

"Who else? I turned off a voice modifier."

Flint laughed. "We're increasing speed. Is Councilman Zorus well?"

Coal's smile faded. "We were separated and I'm alone."

"Damn. We'll talk when we dock with you. I take it we have permission?"

"Granted. I'll slow to a stop when we meet up."

"Glad to hear your voice."

"Yours as well." Coal turned off communications.

Jill blinked back tears, not wanting Coal to see how upset it made her that he'd found his friends. She'd been sure they had more time together. She knew they had mere minutes left before the fast-approaching ships reached them. Her gaze shifted to find Coal silently watching her.

"There's no need for fear. You are safe and my people will not harm you. I am keeping my word to return the shuttle and droids back to your control."

She nodded, her throat too choked with emotion to dare speak for fear of revealing her feelings. It would be better if he assumed she worried about her fate.

Coal rose to his feet, hovering over her, and then he pulled her into his arms. "It will be fine. Don't worry."

The feel of his arms holding her, his wonderful masculine scent and hot skin pressed against her cheek would be sorely missed. She hugged him back, hoping she didn't cling too tightly. She nodded rather than speak.

His hands gently rubbed her lower back through her shirt. "They may seem frightening but know I'd never allow anyone to hurt you."

She nodded again.

"Let me dock to them and then we'll greet them in the cargo hold."

"Okay," she said softly, making her arms release him although she regretted doing it. She stepped away to give him room to move.

Coal dropped back into the pilot seat, his full focus on the controls. She took the time to compose her unstable emotions. She never touched any of the strong booze her father's crew had kept onboard but after Coal left, she'd need it. Getting drunk would be the only thing that might keep her from attempting to follow him to whatever system he lived in just for a chance of a not-so-accidental meeting with him in the near future.

"We're slowing and turning for a soft dock," he informed her minutes later.

"Their ships must really move fast to reach us so quickly." *Lame response*, she berated silently. *But it beats me begging him to open fire on his friends, disabling their ships long enough for us to full burn so we can run away from them.*

The shuttle bumped into something softly, the deck of the floor vibrating slightly, and she knew they'd docked. Coal grinned when he shut down the engines. He stood and turned to address Fray.

"Stand down and order the other droids that guests are boarding. They pose no danger to anything on the shuttle. I want the three of you to shut down until I give further orders."

Fray nodded. "I will relay the order." He claimed the pilot seat.

Coal held out his hand to Jill. "Come with me. Until they realize you are a friend do not make any sudden movements. Just stay at my side."

"Okay." She tried to push down the fear that had her heart racing slightly. *Coal happened to be a sweetheart but what if the other cyborgs weren't?* That silent question left her definitely disturbed. She repeated it aloud.

His squeezed her hand reassuringly. "I gave you my word to free you without harm and they will have to honor it."

That didn't set her at ease by much but, despite her misgivings, she followed alongside him when he moved toward the door. Her dread rose with each step until she fought the urge to flee to her quarters to hide there until after Coal left. His firm hold on her hand kept her at his side though. He walked to exterior loading door and released the lock. The door slid open.

Four tall cyborgs stood waiting on the other side in the docking sleeve attached to the *Jenny*. All of them wore tight, black leather uniforms that covered their bodies from their gray-colored throats to their kickass, military-style, matching black boots. The man in the lead had jet-black hair that fell to his wide, gigantic shoulders but his bright, piercing blue eyes captured Jill's attention the most. His gaze pinned her where she stood.

"This is Jill," Coal's voice deepened. "She rescued me. She's our friend."

The big, scary cyborg shifted his intense gaze from hers to stare calmly at Coal. "She located and took the pod aboard?" He glanced around the cargo hold. "What happened to Councilman Zorus then?" He frowned at Coal after visually searching the area.

"The life pod is on a damaged cargo freighter. The crew picked us up from space and separated him from me." Anger tightened Coal's voice. "The humans who found us weren't friendly. Jill is a trader who came aboard their freighter where they held me captive and she stole me away from them. When they came after us I made certain not to blow them up for fear Zorus remained onboard. I didn't want to accidentally kill him along with the human crew. I have memorized the coordinates of their last location to give you to search their ship for him. I doubt they've traveled far, taking into consideration the damage I caused their engines." He paused. "I wasn't able to go after him myself. Jill's ship is severely outdated, slow, and I needed more men for the odds of a successful rescue to be favorable."

"Um…" Jill whispered and she cleared her throat, trying to speak louder. Five pairs of cyborg eyes turned on her. She looked up at Coal since he didn't scare her. "That captain of the freighter mentioned another cyborg but I forgot about it until this moment. He said Earth Government sent a ship and they took him. The crew hid you to keep them from taking you as well. Your friend is probably either on his way to Earth or already there. I have no idea how long you were with them and the captain didn't say when it happened."

Coal winced, his thumb stroking the back of her hand while he gazed at her. "You're sure?"

"Captain Raul told me he decided to keep you because you looked meaner for fighting on Arris. He said the other one looked kind of pretty and didn't look as though he'd fought much. It really pissed him off that Earth Government had taken your friend without even paying him for finding a cyborg. He seemed sure a reward should have been paid."

"Damn," one of the cyborgs muttered. "Well, we tried. If he's reached Earth, he's lost to us forever. What a shame that is." He chuckled. "Poor them. Imagine his temperament after being around what he hates most."

"Sky," Flint turned his head to shoot an irritated look at a gray-haired cyborg with really scary, unusually pale-blue eyes that had an odd look to them. "We still have to attempt to retrieve him. I'm not fond of the councilman either but he's one of our brothers. He also knows everything about us. They could torture him until his mind snaps and then he might give them all the information they wish to gain about us."

"Or," Sky grinned widely. "They'll believe he's an example of what we've become and decide we're too damn sadistic to fuck with. If anyone could make Earth decide to avoid cyborgs at any cost, it would be Zorus. I know, after spending time with him, that I would do nearly anything to avoid further contact."

A dark-haired cyborg laughed. "He makes a valid point, Flint."

Annoyance flashed on Flint's face. "Don't encourage him, Onyx." He turned to face Sky. "You know more about humans than anyone. How would we obtain him from Earth Government? I need solutions instead of snide comments. Shut off your personality traits this instant and answer me. That's a direct order."

The cyborg sobered, his pale, strange eyes locking with Flint's. "First we'd have to locate where they sent him. They could be keeping him prisoner on one of their war vessels but my estimation would be that they wouldn't wish him contained near all that technology with his active implants. On a ship they couldn't effectively shield all the access points to the main computers. If it were me, I'd keep him drugged while transporting him to a secure location on Earth where they could restrict his abilities. Their smartest move would be to hold him in one of the detention centers where they kept us once if any of them are still operational. We know the locations of them if that's what they've done. It's also logical they wouldn't believe we'd willingly risk returning to Earth under any circumstances to retrieve him. It means surprise would be in our favor."

"If he's there, what is next? Hacking into their security systems to find him shouldn't be too difficult. Humans were always too dependent on them to store all their information." Flint took a deep breath. "It's getting on and off Earth to break him out that will provide a challenge."

"We can't take the *Star* or the *Rally* within range of Earth. They obviously know we didn't legally obtain them after that insurance company tried to retrieve one of them once. They'd send a battle cruiser to intercept us as soon as we entered the system."

Flint's blue gaze locked on Jill. "Coal did say she's in the trading business. We could use this shuttle to reach Earth without triggering alarm. They allow Earth ships to land on the planet."

Jill's mouth dropped open in astonishment. An instant protest formed but she never got the words out. Coal released her hand and stepped in front of her to block the stare of the other cyborg.

"No. She believes Earth Government has a warrant issued for her arrest. She once had a run-in with a few of them. I won't put her at risk in any way. Think of something else, Flint. She saved my life and I gave her my word no harm would come to her."

"Belief and fact are not the same." Flint's voice grew cold. "Rescuing Councilman Zorus is paramount."

"Not to me." Coal's body tensed, his arms tightening until the ridges of muscle seemed to strain. "Her safety and wellbeing are my priority."

Jill inched to the left a little to peer at the four cyborgs facing off against Coal. Flint had an angry frown fixed on his features and his eyes seemed to darken. He held Coal's gaze, never even glancing her way, and then crossed his arms.

"I sympathize. I don't wish any harm to come to the female but we must go after Zorus."

"Find another way." Coal's deep voice sounded his anger. "She's done enough already to risk her life for a cyborg. That freighter came after this shuttle intent on killing her for taking me away from them. She had no reason to do what she did yet she still stole me from them. I'm sure they reported my theft to Earth Government."

"That wouldn't be logical," Sky spoke. "She stated the captain of the freighter didn't hand you over to the authorities and hid your existence. It would be detrimental for them to admit they'd done that. They can't report a theft of something they refused to state they were in possession of in the first place."

Flint frowned at Jill. "Why do you believe you're wanted by Earth Government?"

She hesitated. "About ten months ago I did a trade with a small government outpost. They realized I didn't have a crew and decided they could force me to return the payment they'd made, figuring they could pocket it themselves, and wanted to sell me into one of the nearby whorehouse ships to gain some extra profit. I wasn't stupid enough not to go in armed and managed to get to my shuttle. They followed me straight into an asteroid field. I couldn't outrun them, they were gaining on me, and I'd grown desperate enough to fly into it, thinking they wouldn't follow. They did. Their newer shuttle didn't have as much shielding as these older models, which have it to make up for the sluggish navigational controls. They blew up after a few direct hits from the asteroids while I just suffered a lot of dents to the hull. I'm sure they reported it before they came after me."

Sky shook his head. "It sounds as if they were attempting to steal money from the government and ruin a trade contact. They wouldn't have reported any illegal actions they took to their superiors. It would be foolish. We know enough about Earth Government to be certain they would have taken swift action to make an example out of their men for disobeying their code of conduct."

"They search all incoming and outgoing vessels that want to land on Earth," she warned them. "Even if I'm not wanted, there's no way to get you to the surface undetected. They'd board the *Jenny* and find you when they scan it for illegal contraband. It's protocol to do that to anything incoming."

"I'm not risking her life." Coal shook his head and directed a furious glare at Flint. "Your argument isn't valid, considering humans are not known for being logical. She could very well be wanted by Earth Government and therefore, that is putting her at risk of arrest or death."

Flint took a deep breath and said, "I see. She means something to you."

Coal jerked his head. "She does."

Jill's heart soared when he said the words but his next ones left her feeling cold.

"I gave her my word that I'd release her shuttle as soon as I found you. I swore on my honor no harm would come to her. She had no reason to take me from the humans who abused me, yet she did. We owe her a debt we will not repay by putting her in danger."

"No one is mentioning that she's seen us and knows of our existence," one of the cyborgs standing in the back by the docking doors said softly. "You shouldn't have promised to release her, Coal. She knows too much to safely allow her to go free."

Fear inched up Jill's spine and she subconsciously moved closer to Coal, her hand touching his back. He didn't glance at her but his hand reached back, wrapping around her hip, and tugged her behind his body until only her head peeked out from behind him.

"I will fight anyone who attempts to harm her," Coal snarled. "She goes free. She isn't an enemy of our people."

"Easy," Flint's tone softened. "Stand down, Coal. We won't harm the female in any way." He shot a glare at the cyborg who'd suggested they not release Jill. "Earth Government has got living proof that some of us survived when they took possession of Councilman Zorus. It's irrelevant if she were to make a statement to them now that she'd been in contact with a group of us. When we attempt to retrieve him from them they are sure to understand he's not the only surviving cyborg."

"She could warn them we are coming."

Jill opened her mouth to deny it but Coal spoke first.

"She would not do that."

Sky sighed. "It would be a hell of a way for her to get them to drop an arrest warrant on her if she bargained that information with them."

Coal growled, his body trembling. "She is not our enemy. She risked her life and her shuttle to rescue me."

The gray-haired cyborg threw up his hands. "Don't shoot the messenger. I'm just stating the obvious, man. I had to say it since Flint ordered me to be all logical. I didn't say I believe it but it is an option we have to consider."

Flint sighed loudly. "Agreed." He turned toward Coal. "I have a solution. One of our men will remain with the female to monitor her transmissions until after we've rescued councilman Zorus. She will be safe, unharmed, and it should only take us a matter of days to execute a plan to retrieve him. We will allow her to go free when we pick up the male assigned to stay with her."

Coal's mouth opened but Flint cut him off.

"We'll pay her generously for her time to compensate her for the days she is detained here. This is a safe location for her shuttle, she is far from Earth, and we scanned the area. No other ships are within range. That's a fair resolution, Coal. You can't disagree with the logic of it."

Coal's body relaxed and his grip on her hip eased. "I want your word of honor that no harm will come to her, Flint."

"You have my word, Coal. I'm fond of human females, if you will remember." He smiled. "I joined a family unit with one. I'll have her treated the way I would my Mira."

* * * * *

Coal stared deeply into Flint's eyes and nodded. "I believe you." He turned his head to look down at Jill. She appeared paler than normal. "Is this agreeable to you?"

147

She hesitated and her hand on the small of his back eased but she didn't pull it away. "I trust you. It sounds reasonable since I get why they'd be worried. They don't know me."

He nodded before meeting Flint's waiting gaze. "I'll remain with her." He resisted smiling. While he experienced elation at being back with his cyborg brothers he didn't want to say goodbye to Jill. The thought of never seeing her again made him ache in his chest and suffer depressed feelings.

Flint jerked his head, moving toward a corner. Coal hesitated before following him, not wanting to break the physical contact with Jill but realized Flint wished to speak to him privately. He faced Flint when both men stood far from the others.

Flint's voice lowered. "I'd feel better if Onyx stayed. I'm aware you're sensitive about the damage you suffered but there's no way for you to constantly monitor this shuttle. I know you don't have the ability to control your emotions or thought processes but please attempt to right now. He will follow my orders, he won't harm her in the least, and he can make certain she is unable to send a warning to Earth. With his implants, he will uplink to the onboard computer to block all transmissions. I'm sorry."

"Jill wouldn't do that." Coal's temper flared. "I trust her with my life."

"I don't know her and it's not just your life at risk."

He hated logic at that moment but he couldn't deny Flint had valid points. "I'll stay as well then. Onyx can monitor all communications and I'll finish some repairs on the shuttle I wished to do for Jill as repayment for saving me."

Flint shook his head, his gaze softening. "You're very protective of her, Coal. I'd go so far as to state you're unstable. It's not a surprise after everything that has been done to you and all you've had to endure. I need to know if you've asked her to join a family unit with you. I saw the way she touched you and the way you touched her. Say so now if that happened."

He fought the temptation to lie. "I haven't."

Flint nodded. "I'm ordering you to return to the *Star* then. Onyx will be assigned to stay here. I'll make it very clear that he isn't to harm her in any way."

Coal's breath seemed to freeze in his chest at the idea of leaving Jill. He turned his head, meeting her curious gaze across the cargo hold, but he didn't see any indication she felt fear for the cyborgs around her. His attention shifted to Onyx. The man openly stared at Jill with interest but he saw no animosity toward the human. As a matter of fact, Onyx's gaze drifted up and down Jill's form, taking in every inch of her body while Coal watched. Anger and a sudden urge to go punch the other male gripped him hard. Onyx's gaze had definitely stalled upon Jill's breasts to linger there longer than necessary to assess her.

"Coal?" Flint gripped his arm.

"What?" Coal tore his glare from Onyx. His voice came out harsher than he meant it to and he realized his hands were fisted.

"Return to the *Star*. I swear the female will be fine."

"I have to return control of her droids to her. I had her give me total control of them."

149

"Onyx will hack them and do that when we pick him up on the return trip to Garden. You turning over control to her would be a useless waste of your time since he'll have to do that anyway. Say goodbye now and leave. We need to rescue the councilman as quickly as possible. We can't remain here any longer."

Anguish gripped Coal. He nodded, knowing he had no other recourse.

Chapter Nine

Jill knew when Coal walked toward her with his grim expression that he'd say goodbye to her. She could see it in the way his shoulders sagged and she swore she even saw sadness dulling his beautiful dark gaze. She fought to hold back tears while stiffening her spine. *Life sucks.*

He stopped in front of her. "I've been ordered to return to one of the other ships. Onyx will remain with you. Flint is, at this moment, ordering him to treat you very well. He won't harm you, Jill. You will be safe. If I didn't know that with certainty, I wouldn't have agreed to allow him to remain."

She couldn't find her voice around the emotion that choked her. Regret, heartbreak, and the desire to beg him not to go all mixed together until she didn't know which one she felt the strongest.

"Thank you for deciding to risk your life to save mine. You're unique and wonderful for a human."

Damn, I'm going to cry, she thought, still fighting the urge hard. "Thanks," she whispered. "You're pretty unique and wonderful too." She forced a smile she didn't feel. "For a cyborg."

He didn't laugh. "I wish I could have fixed you." His voice lowered. "The lessons weren't completed but I hope you remember them."

"I always will," she swore sincerely. There would never be a day that passed when she's ever forget touching Coal, his kisses, or the way he'd made her feel when he showed her how wonderful it could be between two people. "I won't ever forget you."

His hand rose but then halted mere inches from her face. "I will never forget you either. I wish we had more time."

"You could stay on the shuttle too." Hope flared inside her. "Two cyborgs watching me are better than one, right?"

His hand dropped to his side. "I asked but Flint has ordered me to return to his ship. I have to go. We need to make our way to Earth to rescue the councilman. The longer they have him at their mercy, the higher the risk that they'll make him talk. He knows too much about my people. Time is of the essence."

"Couldn't you just watch me?" She wasn't willing to give up so easily on any possibility of keeping Coal on the *Jenny*. "I would feel so much safer with you than with a stranger."

"I'm damaged and unable to monitor the shuttle as Onyx is capable of doing. I requested that job but Flint made valid, logical points that I couldn't argue with."

"Coal?" Flint had moved to the docking door. "Let's go."

Coal visually tensed. "I must go." His hand reached for her again, his fingertips brushing her cheek lightly. "Goodbye, Jill. I will think of you very often."

She grabbed his hand when he tried to pull it away, keeping hold of him. Her mind struggled to come up with a way to prolong her time with Coal and she spun, facing the cyborg in charge. "Hang on. May I call you Flint?"

Flint frowned. "Yes. What is it?"

"I have an idea on how to get your Zorus back."

Interest sparked in his eyes. "I'm listening."

She had to release Coal, hated to do it, but she walked closer to the scary, leather-clad cyborg, her mind still running plans through her head, hoping to nail one down.

"I have a few contacts on Earth. That's who I buy my supplies from. I can't shuttle you directly to Earth but I meet up with another trader right on the outer edge of the solar system. Those sellers are real slime balls with no conscience if the price is right. They trust me not to screw them over if I deal with them directly. I would have to go with you, hire them to take you to Earth, and you could just give me the credits to pay them with if you have it. They will do as they are told as long as we make it clear they don't see any of it until you're safely returned."

"Slime balls?" Flint frowned. "What are those?"

"See what I deal with?" Sky chuckled when Jill glanced at him and he winked at her. He shook his head, shooting Flint an exasperated look. "It is a term humans use for unsavory characters. She's saying that, for the right price, they'd kill their own family members but we could bribe them easily to do whatever we require. I also have to admit I like her plan better than anything I've thought up so far."

Coal gripped her arm from behind, spun her around, and stared hard at her, an angry expression on his handsome face. "That would put you at risk. You'd be too close to Earth."

"I go that close every time I have to resupply and I haven't been caught yet."

He hesitated. "Your line of work is far too dangerous."

"I know." She smiled, happy that her plan gave her a chance to keep company with Coal longer. "But it's useful right now since it really could work. They could fly right to the surface of Earth and then take off again without being searched. I'm sure they know which officials to bribe to look the other way. They sell me all kinds of illegal goods they smuggle past the checkpoints."

"How do we know these slime balls won't see us, realize what we are, and try to cash in a reward with Earth Government?"

The cyborg named Onyx really had a talent for annoying Jill. She eased out of Coal's hold and turned to face the jerk. She shot him a dirty look. "I'll tell them what Earth Government did to that captain of the freighter who had Zorus. They just took your friend away from that ship without paying them a single credit and threatened to blow it up his they tried to stop them."

She turned to Flint then. "These guys I buy from will believe me. If there's a way for the government to rip people off, we all know they will. I have no idea how much you know about Earth these days but the government has become so corrupt it's not funny. Nobody trusts what they say and it's a joy to most to screw them over if given the opportunity. These guys may even give you a discount on doing this job if you stress how badly it will piss off the high-ranking officials on Earth to steal your friend back."

Flint glanced at Sky. "You're our expert. Is she correct?"

"She's right." Sky flashed a grin. "Humans are more likely to trust the contacts they make over anything Earth Government states. There's an honor code amongst thieves."

"I'm not a thief," Jill protested. "But I do trade with them."

Sky chuckled. "My apologies. There's an honor code amongst criminals."

She couldn't deny that. Technically she would be considered one for knowingly buying illegal goods and it could be debatable if she fit the thief category after she'd stolen Coal. "Apology accepted."

"Fine." Flint took a deep breath. "Your shuttle is too slow but we don't want to alarm them with you meeting them in an unfamiliar one. We'll dock your shuttle inside one of the cargo bays aboard the *Star* and transport it closer to Earth. At that point we'll fly it to meet up with your contacts."

She nodded. "Sounds good."

"You'll remain on your shuttle and Onyx will remain with you to make certain you don't change your mind about helping us."

Damn! She tried to hide her disappointment. An idea struck though. "Coal promised to help me do some repairs that need to be done. I'd feel better if he's here since I don't know your guy." She shot Onyx a glower and then looked back at Flint. "I'm fine with Onyx staying but I'd rather not be alone with him. I don't think it's too much to ask to allow Coal to stay with me, considering I'm risking my ass to help you. I don't even want to be paid for my time."

Flint studied her for long seconds. "Fine. Coal may stay aboard. Onyx," he looked away from her, "park this in cargo bay two. You have control of her shuttle while Coal helps her with whatever repairs are needed." He met Coal's gaze. "Is that agreeable to you?"

Coal didn't hesitate. "Yes."

"Fine. We'll meet again to discuss the exact plan before we reach the edge of the solar system containing Earth." He strode to the docking sleeve. "Let's go," he ordered.

Onyx frowned when the cyborgs exited her shuttle. He sealed the cargo door closed, his attention shifting from Jill to Coal. "What kind of outdated system am I dealing with? It's fine with me if you want to pilot the shuttle while I remain with her."

Coal glared at the other man. "You heard Flint. Do your job and I'll do mine."

"You've already piloted this piece of junk. You're familiar with it and I'm sure you wish to be helpful. Go dock us inside the cargo bay."

Coal didn't say a word but shook his head, not moving an inch toward the door. They watched each other. Jill had no idea what the problem between the two men happened to be, not knowing their history, but the tension became obvious. She cleared her throat.

"Coal?"

He tore his glare away from the other man. His features softened when he looked down at her. "Yes, Jill?"

"Why don't you help me? I'm sure your friend can find his way to the pilot seat."

"I've already linked to your computer." Onyx grimaced. "It's barbaric."

The engines roared to life, startling Jill enough that she nearly tripped when she jumped. Coal's steadied her with his lightning quick reflexes.

"Don't be alarmed. He doesn't actually have to walk there to steer the shuttle." He kept his tone low. "He has active, working implants and is able to do things I can't."

"Should we warn him about the stabilizers?" she whispered.

Coal grinned, shaking his head. "It will be a surprise for him," he whispered back. He moved her closer to a bulkhead, leaning against it but still holding her arms. "I'm guessing they will make for a rough landing."

Jill nodded. "Expect a hard drop. The sensors are about four feet over what they read. He'll be told by the computer it's four inches."

"What are you discussing?" Onyx irritated tone couldn't be mistaken.

"We're talking about things that don't work right on the shuttle," Jill answered honestly, talking louder, and kept her back to him for fear of laughing. "There are a lot of things that need to be repaired."

"I'm sure of that fact." Onyx sounded closer. "This shuttle should have been decommissioned a good decade ago. It's amazing it's still functioning. We'd be kind if we blew it up for you and left you on Earth. They have opened the cargo bay doors." He paused. "We're setting down now."

Coal suddenly wrapped his arms around her hips and jerked her off the floor. Her chest smashed against his as the *Jenny's* engines cut out. Coal's body tensed, his knees bending slightly to brace their combined weight, and then the sick sensation of falling made Jill's stomach feel like it rose into her throat. The belly of the shuttle slammed into something solid. The entire ship groaned.

Coal straightened his legs to return to his full height, chuckled, and eased Jill down the front of his body until her feet returned to the floor. She grinned back at him. He'd been so sweet to use his own body to cushion hers from the impact. From behind her she heard a string of curses and turned her head. Onyx lay sprawled on his side, struggling to sit up in the middle of the cargo hold.

"I assume your piloting skills need finer tuning." Coal laughed.

"The sensors are incorrect," Onyx hissed, sitting on his ass on the deck. He glared at both of them. "You knew and didn't tell me. You had no right to do that. I'm ordering you to return to the *Star*."

Coal's humor died. "You had no right to stare at Jill's body the way I caught you doing. If you believe you are going to get an opportunity to be alone with her, you are wrong. You also have no authority to give me orders."

Onyx stood. "I heard you were damaged but you're insane as well."

Coal took a step closer to the other cyborg. "I saw the way you stared at her breasts and I didn't misread your offer for me to pilot the shuttle as an excuse to give you the ability to be alone with Jill."

Shock had kept Jill frozen at Coal's sudden outburst until he moved again, his intent to attack clear. She lunged, grabbed hold of his waist to block him from going after the other cyborg, and clung to him.

"Calm down," she ordered him.

Coal continued to glare at the other cyborg but he didn't attempt to remove her from his path to the other cyborg. Jill turned her head, glaring at Onyx.

"You've got permission to stay on my shuttle but get out of my cargo hold now. You can stay somewhere else."

Onyx glared at Jill. "You don't give me orders, female."

She clenched her teeth and focused on Coal. "Hey."

He looked down at her, still enraged, and said, "He wants to touch you. He's attracted to you."

He's jealous, she realized. It stunned her but then warmth flooded her in all the good ways. "You need to calm down. Let's take a walk together since he won't leave."

Coal took a deep breath. "Fine." His body relaxed but only slightly. He glared at Onyx again. "You stay away from Jill. She isn't interested in intercourse with you."

"How would you know?" Onyx's tone turned cold. "I've cataloged all entries stored in the ship's logs and she has few communications with males, none of them of a personal nature, and logic states she has no male in her life to tend to her basic needs."

"I'm the only male she'll allow to touch her."

Okay, Jill thought, understanding that Coal obviously didn't have a problem letting the other guy know they were getting it on. She tugged at him. "Let's go to my quarters."

Coal nodded and drew his heated gaze from the now-mute cyborg. Coal took her hand and headed for the door of the cargo hold. Jill had to jog to keep up.

They didn't talk until the doors to her room securely closed behind them. Coal stopped by the bed, released her hand, and spun to face her. He still looked pretty angry.

"He wants to put his hands on you. Cyborgs have basic needs, there are no unattached females traveling with them, and you are not to be alone with him, Jill. He will attempt to seduce you into agreeing to allow him to take you to bed."

"You're jealous," she informed him softly.

Some of his anger seeped out. "I believe I am. I feel rage over him wanting to touch you and possessive of you at the same time." He took a deep breath, his broad chest expanding. "I have felt possessive of you before but this is stronger."

Jill bit her lower lip and then stepped forward. "What else do you feel?"

"I didn't wish to leave you. I'm…relieved we are together still. My chest began to ache painfully when I believed I wouldn't see you again."

Tears filled her eyes and she blinked them back but more surfaced.

"I don't mean to upset you. Have I made you feel sadness? I know I'm damaged and unable to control the ability to suppress emotions."

"Not all tears are from negative emotions."

"Which ones would cause tears that are positive?"

Jill hesitated. "Relief, happiness, just to name a few."

"Why would you feel those things when I say I don't want to leave you?"

"I don't want to say goodbye to you either." She reached out for him, cupping his face, and drew it closer to hers. "I'm going to miss you desperately when you leave me."

Surprise flickered on his handsome face and then his lips were on hers. His tongue delved inside, sweeping across hers. He gripped her with both of his hands and her feet left the floor slowly while Coal lifted her higher up his body to align their faces better, to deepen the kiss.

Longing and passion swamped Jill. Her hands slid from his cheeks to his throat and then her arms wrapped around him tightly, clinging. Coal turned them and then her back gently bumped the wall. He adjusted his hold on her until he held her weight with one arm around her waist. His free hand tore at the fastening of her pants, opened them, and then shoved them down her dangling legs.

It wasn't easy—she was concentrating on his kisses—but she wiggled her hips and kicked enough to help him get them down her legs. Her boots slipped off her feet when he stepped on the material and then jerked her higher to free her of everything. Jill automatically locked her thighs around his hips. The arm around her back moved under her ass, pushing her higher until she knew she dampened his belly from the proof of how turned on he made her. A moan tore from her throat as she rubbed her spread pussy against his skin, eager to feel him touching her there, not caring what part of him did. The sound of material tearing barely registered.

The arm shelving her ass adjusted her lower body and then she moaned loudly against his driving tongue when Coal's thick, hard cock nudged the lips of her sex, sliding a little on the soaked need there, before he drove home. The feel of him entering her pussy, stretching her, and

161

filling her had her crying out. Their lips parted, both of them panting, and their gazes locked.

"I want you more than anything I've ever desired," Coal growled. "You are what I imagine pure joy is when I am with you."

"I feel the same," she admitted, not caring at that moment if he realized she loved him.

She used her arms, braced on his shoulders, to lift a little and then drop, taking more of his cock until she felt completely impaled by him. They both softly groaned at the feeling of him that deep inside her, her vaginal muscles gripping him tightly. Coal took over then, pinning her tighter to the wall, and started to drive up inside her. His powerful body held her still while his hips thrust hard and deep, creating intense ecstasy as they clung to each other, their gazes fused. It built into pure frenzy.

"Come for me," Coal snarled. "I can't hold off."

He pounded harder, faster, wilder, and the rapture of the rapid friction their bodies shared became too much. Jill's eyes closed, unable to keep them open anymore, her mouth parted, and she threw her face against the curve of his chest where it met his shoulder. Her teeth sank into his skin. His entire body started to violently shake and that did it for Jill. She screamed out when raw pleasure tore through her body, her mind shutting down from overload. She heard Coal shout her name, his body nearly crushing her against the wall, and they both trembled together until everything stilled but their pounding hearts and heavy breathing.

He eased Jill away from the wall, still holding her tightly, their bodies still linked, and backed up. He reached behind him where her legs wrapped

162

around his hips and lifted them a little higher then he slowly sat on the bed with her on his lap.

"Jill?"

She licked her lips, opened her eyes, and saw a red mark on his skin where she'd left teeth impressions. "I'm so sorry." She jerked back to stare at him in shock. "I didn't mean to bite you."

A wide grin spread across his striking face. "I enjoyed it."

Truth shone in his incredibly sexy gaze. She smiled. "That was amazing."

"Jill?" He took a deep breath. "Come with me."

"I just did." She grinned.

Amusement sparked in his gaze and his arms tightened around her, hugging her. "I mean when this is over I want you to remain with me. I enjoyed my time in space with my fellow cyborgs but I miss being on a planet. I wish to return to the one where my people have made a new home and I want you to go with me."

Her breath caught as understanding hit. Her mouth opened but nothing came out.

"Did you hear me? Will you at least consider it? There's room on the *Star* to keep your *Jenny* to transport it to my planet, Garden. You don't have to give up your shuttle or your droids. If you don't wish to live in space anymore we, my people, have settled on a planet comparable to Earth. If you wish to remain in space, I would agree to do that as well. As long as we remain together it doesn't matter where we are."

So many thoughts and emotions crowded her mind that it left her speechless. Most of all she had to fight the urge to burst into tears. He wanted to stay with her! Pure joy filled her and she opened her mouth to tell him yes.

"Think about it, Jill." He gave her a tense smile. "Do not answer me right now. We both need time to carefully weigh all our options and make certain this is what we both want. In a few days we'll discuss this again when the idea of staying together isn't so new."

She hoped he wasn't reconsidering asking her. She forced air into her lungs, silently praying he hadn't just asked her to share a life with him in the heat of the moment after awesome sex. If he changed his mind it would tear her apart inside. A few days to think on it for both of them probably would be the smart thing to do and Coal's cyborg mind probably needed that time to be certain of his decision.

"Okay."

The speaker in her room made a crackling noise and then Onyx's voice sounded. "Jill? Flint wishes you to come send a communication to your contact on Earth. He spoke to the council and they feel it's important to set this plan in motion before we reach the edge of Earth's solar system. They ran the odds and believe it's better to avoid extra days that Councilman Zorus might be tortured."

She smiled at Coal, wiggling on his lap. "Okay. I'll meet you in the piloting station in about five minutes. I take it you want to monitor everything I say?"

"Affirmative," Onyx replied. "Money isn't an issue and you are cleared to offer as much of it as you believe will get the job done."

"Awesome. Cut the coms and I'll see you in five."

The speaker clicked again. Coal's features hardened. "How dangerous is this?"

She hesitated. "I've dealt with David, my supplier, half a dozen times. I wouldn't turn my back on him but he's never tried to screw me."

Anger flashed on his handsome face. "He better not attempt to share intercourse with you."

Laughing, Jill wiggled again, separating their bodies, and got to her feet. "Not that kind of screwing. He's never tried to kill me or not give me a shipment of goods I paid for. That's what I meant. Let's get cleaned up and make this communication call."

Coal nodded. "I need to send a communication of my own." He fingered the torn material on his pants. He'd obviously ripped them open rather than taking the time to unfasten them when he'd been eager to fuck her. "This was the last pair of pants I could fit into. I need to request clothing be sent to me."

Jill laughed. "I have some stretchy sweatpants you could wear." Her gaze paused on his chest. "But none of my shirts would fit you. I'm kind of glad about that."

"You don't wish me to stretch out your shirts? My upper body is quite larger than yours."

"No. I just enjoy seeing your sexy chest." She winked, moving toward the corner cleansing foam unit. "Our minutes are ticking by. Come on. It will be a tight fit but we can share. It will be faster."

Coal didn't move to join her. "If I go into that small space with you naked I will take you again."

Jill's body responded instantly. "I don't care if Onyx has to wait a little longer for us to show up to make that call."

"Flint would mind. I don't want him believing me being with you is interfering with his mission. He could order us apart until it is over."

That killed the lust that had sparked in Jill. "The pants are in the lowest drawer in the corner. I'll hurry." She spun away, vowing to take the fastest cleansing of her life. No way did she want Flint ordering Coal to return to the *Star*.

Chapter Ten

"Coal, I've come to a decision," she said softly, meeting his gaze over the air cleaner module he worked on.

His gaze lifted, met hers. "I want you to be certain. We had this discussion two days ago when you said you had an answer for me. You have many things to consider. It's an emotional risk as well and I demand you take more time before you make such a life-altering decision."

Frustration rose. "Damn it, Coal. I keep trying to tell you—"

"Give it more time. I don't want to rush you."

"But—"

"Jill," he cut her off again. "I demand you take this time to consider it very carefully to avoid rushing into a decision you may later regret."

"Have you changed your mind about wanting me in your life long term?"

He gently placed the tool he gripped on the casing of the unit. His mouth was grim. "Why would you come to that incorrect conclusion?"

"You won't listen to me when I tell you I know what I want to do. Every time I try to tell you, you cut me off or walk away. If you didn't mean it, if you asked in haste, and you've decided it wasn't such a good idea now that we're not all hot and sweaty after sex, just say it. I'm getting really frustrated with you shutting me down."

Coal rose to his feet and stepped around the obstacle between them. He crouched down next to her side, the black leather outfit he wore now made a slight squeaking noise. He nearly touched her but kept a few inches separating their bodies. His gaze held hers.

"I'm afraid you will say no and I am not ready to hear it if that is your answer. Every moment we spend together gives me hope I can convince you I'm worthy of you giving up the way of life you've become accustomed to. You won't be able to continue to trade if you decide to join a family unit with me. I'm a cyborg and, as you once told me, traders would get a high price for me and it would put you at high risk every time you came into contact with them because they'd attempt to take me from the *Jenny*. The only thing I've changed my mind about is offering to remain in space with you. We need to live on a planet where you're safe."

Her eyebrows rose. She didn't care where they lived as long as they were together. The only thing he'd said that had her reeling were three words. "A family unit?"

He scowled suddenly. "Of course. I am that serious about you. Did you believe I'd ask you to give up everything and offer you nothing in return? It's the equivalence of marriage, to my people. It's a deep commitment we would make to one another."

Tears blinded her. "You're asking me to marry you?"

He closed his eyes. "This is why I wish to delay your answer. I've upset you."

She turned and her knee bumped his inner thigh as she gripped his leather shirt. She didn't like the outfit all the cyborgs wore. She preferred him walking around shirtless in ill-fitting pants. She wanted to touch his hot, bare skin rather than the thick leather her fingers clutched.

"Yes."

Dark eyes snapped open to stare at her uncomprehendingly.

"Yes. I'll marry you or be a family unit with you, whatever you want to call it, but yes!"

A grin slowly spread across his handsome face. "Yes?"

She nodded, grinning back. "Hell yes. Is that better?"

He sucked in air, his chest expanding. "Are you sure? It is a lot for you to give up for me."

"It's not. You said I could keep the *Jenny* and my guys. Trading?" She snorted. "I hated that job and I sure won't miss dealing with all the lowlife creeps I've had to put up with. I have no idea what I'll do now to help support us on your planet but a year ago I never saw myself in this line of work. I'll adjust and we'll have each other. That's all that matters to me."

Coal's body slid forward until his knees hit the deck. "You're one hundred percent certain? I don't want to feel this happiness only to have it torn away if you change your mind."

Jill lifted her boot over one of his thighs and scooted off her seat, right onto his lap, her legs wrapping around his hips. His hands gripped her ass, holding her in place, and she grinned at him.

"I've never been surer of anything in my life."

"I'll fill out the paperwork immediately and transmit it to Garden." His grin widened even more. "They won't refuse my request to form a family unit with you. Because of my history of abuse at the hands of the cyborg females I am permitted special consideration."

"I don't know what that means but as long as they allow it, great."

He chuckled. "They will allow it."

"So do we have a ceremony?"

"We could if you wish but it just involves putting in a request, being approved, and then I need to sign the agreement. There's no need for you to worry about a job. I will take care of you and your way of thinking in terms of financial issues is irrelevant with my people. We don't have a monetary system on Garden."

"Coal, I have something to tell you."

His features froze and the smile died. "What is it?"

He braced for bad news. It was so obvious that Jill had to resist grinning at the humor of the situation, considering what she wanted to share with him hopefully would be the exact opposite.

"I'm in love with you."

He gaped at her and then, to her utter surprise, tears filled his eyes, slid down both cheeks, and his hands slid from her ass. If it wasn't for her fingers gripping his shirt and her legs secured around his hips she would have hit the deck. His body seemed to totally go lax until he swayed where he crouched on his knees.

"Coal?" Alarm gripped her. "Are you all right? Did I say something wrong? Speak to me."

He suddenly moved, his arms wrapping around her, and she gasped when her body ended up smashed tightly against his when he roughly jerked her against him. He clutched her so firmly she could barely breathe, his face pressing tightly into the cradle of her shoulder and neck. His hot tears wet her shirt.

She clung to him, had to fight to free her hands, trapped between their chests, to wrap them around his ribs to his back. Her arms held him as hard as she could, hugging him.

"Coal?"

He just held her for a good minute until some of the tension left in his body and his fierce hold on her eased slightly. He lifted his head, his dark eyes still swimming with tears when she met his gaze.

"I didn't mean to upset you, honey."

He slowly smiled. "You love me."

Jill studied him closely, seeing happiness through his tears, and nodded. "I really do love you. I didn't mean to make you cry."

One of his arms released her and he tentatively touched his face, wiping at the wetness that he discovered there, seeming shocked at the tears. His cheeks seemed to darken slightly and then his smile widened.

"I'm happy."

Jill blinked rapidly. "I'm so glad to hear that."

"I believe I'm in love with you too. I'm not sure exactly what love is but you are everything to me, Jill. My chest hurts right now and I can't stop the tears. I feel that much joy."

"Oh hell," she muttered, letting her own tears fall. "That's love, honey. We're in love with each other."

"I'm never going to let you go." He leaned closer until his nose touched hers, staring into her eyes deeply. "I am going to make you as happy as you make me. I will die to protect you."

"What the hell?" A familiar male voice interrupted. "Is everything cool here? What happened? Is someone hurt?"

Coal turned his head and grinned at Sky, who had entered the cargo hold from the *Star* without them hearing him. "She loves me and I love her."

Jill blinked back more tears, turning her head to grin at the gray-haired cyborg who gaped at the both of them. He put his hands on his hips and then flashed them an amused smile.

"I'm glad to hear it. You're a cute couple, though a little wet at the moment. It's a good thing I didn't wait another minute from the way you're wrapped around each other." He chuckled. "I came to tell you that Flint is on his way. We're approaching the edge of the solar system and Jill's contact has been hailing the *Jenny* for the past few minutes. Onyx tried to reach you but you weren't answering your com, Coal. You may want to break it up before Flint thinks he's interrupting you two about to nail each other on the deck there."

Coal frowned. "Why would we do something painful and unusual? I'd never harm Jill."

Jill suddenly laughed. "He means having sex on the floor. Nailing each other is slang for that."

"Yeah. What she said." Sky shook his head. "I swear, I'm going to give a damn class to teach them how to understand Earth lingo."

A chuckle escaped Jill. "Don't. I think it's adorable." She winked at Coal. "You're so cute."

Coal smiled at her. "Really?"

"I think I prefer you grunting and groaning over listening to the lovey-dovey crap." Sky turned his head. "Here comes Flint. I hear his boots. The guy really needs to learn how to walk instead of stomp."

Jill moved first, struggling to unwind her limbs from around Coal. His strong hands gripped her, easing her to her feet before he rose. She wiped at her tears, turning and reaching for Coal's face. He leaned down enough to let her use her thumbs to brush away his tears too. The sounds of something striking the ramp made the three of them turn.

"What is going on?" Flint frowned, coming to a halt just inside the cargo hold, his gaze darting between the three of them.

"They just realized they are in love." Sky chuckled. "And I interrupted them about to have intercourse right there where they are standing."

A blush warmed Jill's cheeks but she met the dark-haired cyborg's gaze without flinching. "Sky said that David has been trying to reach me?"

Flint cleared his throat. "Yes. I had Onyx respond, pretending to be you since you use a voice modifier when speaking to the human males. He's acquired a team to break Councilman Zorus from where he's being kept. They have already located where he is and have hatched a plot to rescue him. Onyx allowed me to listen into the communication and it sounded like a more reasonable, safer solution than sending cyborgs to the planet surface. I had Onyx agree to the plan and the payment they demanded. By tomorrow, Councilman Zorus should be free. The mercenaries hired to retrieve him will meet up with us on your shuttle in two days at the outer edge of the solar system where we'd originally agreed to meet David."

"That's fast." Jill nodded. "I told you David would have contacts on Earth to get stuff done. He probably knows all kinds of thugs. He's got to buy his wares from people who are skilled at stealing stuff to sell the illegal crap he offers. I've even heard of slavers kidnapping women from the surface to sell to the floating whorehouses and it wouldn't surprise me if David sold people too. Paying someone to kidnap a cyborg shouldn't be that much of a stretch for those kinds of creeps."

Flint nodded. "You were correct. He asked for half payment upfront but I remembered your warning not to pay until the mission is complete. He wasn't happy but he agreed to the terms."

"Right." She nodded. "As I said, these guys aren't real trustworthy but when money is involved you can count on them until they are paid."

Coal took a step toward Flint, smiling. "I wish to contact the council to formally request forming a family unit with Jill."

The instant grin softened Flint's normally harsh features. "I'm happy for you and I'm certain they will agree." His gaze flicked to Jill. "Coal has been given special consideration and, as such, there is no breeding pact in his case. That's one big obstacle you will not have to confront."

Confused, Jill glanced up at Coal. "What's that?"

He shook his head, smiling at her. "Something you never have to worry about. You are the only female for me for the rest of my life. I vow total monogamy."

Her eyebrows rose. "I'm glad to hear that and later I'm going to have you explain that to me in detail." She didn't want to have that discussion in front of Sky and Flint. She glanced at the later. "Is it going to be all right with you to haul my shuttle to your planet? I'd like to keep her. I know she's outdated and slow but she's special to me."

"Humans become attached easily to objects," Sky said softly. "That's normal."

Flint shrugged, glancing around the cargo hold. "We have the room. I don't see why not." His gaze fixed on Jill suddenly. "If Coal wishes to return to Garden with you, they will not allow you to fly this back into space. You'll know the location of our home world and therefore pose a risk if you were ever captured by Earth Government. Your shuttle would be flown to the planet surface and the engines decommissioned."

She had to adjust to that little bit of news. Coal moved behind her, his arms wrapping around her waist, and she easily leaned back into his body. She nodded.

"That's okay as long as we're together."

"Good." Flint grinned suddenly, taking another look at the inside of the Jenny. "It is probably safer if you don't continue to fly this thing for much longer. It's very outdated."

"I have a question." Coal hesitated, glancing at Jill and then Flint. "Jill mentioned that she used to live on a farm on Earth. Do you believe the council would allow me to have some of the undeveloped land near the north wall of the city? They've started growing food in that section but it is

175

vast enough that they may not need to use all of it. I don't know how happy Jill will be if we live in the center of the city."

Jill tilted her head up, gazing with love at Coal. "Really? I think I'd love that. I miss trees and fresh air." She paused. "Does your planet have that? We haven't really talked about it. I'm hoping it's not a bio dome similar to the ones on the moon and Saturn."

"It's very similar to Earth," Flint offered with a smile. "There is more water content and less land mass but it's still beautiful where Earth has been overdeveloped. The air is good and the vegetation is lush. The only city on the planet is the one we've built."

"There are no other life forms?" That surprised Jill. If it had an Earth-like environment, then life forms should exist.

"There are plenty of them but we built a wall to surround our city."

"Is what lives there dangerous?" She hoped not.

"Not within our walls. We didn't want to compromise the natural inhabitants or for them to pose a risk to us. It works well." Flint smiled. "I see no reason why the council would oppose it if you chose to live on the outer edge of the city. Perhaps they could put you in charge of some of our agriculture projects."

"I'd enjoy that." Hope shone in Coal's eyes.

"Me too," Jill grinned, memories of her childhood on the farm surfacing. She'd been in space far too long and the idea of fresh air, open land, and vegetation sounded heavenly to her.

"You two have some time to work out all the details." Flint grinned. "For the next day, relax. We're going to fly the *Jenny* out of the cargo bay in the morning to use it for the last part of the trip. The *Star* and the *Rally* will remain here."

"The *Rally*?" Jill hadn't heard that name before.

"It's the smaller ship traveling with the *Star*," Flint explained. We wanted extra weaponry in case we needed it. I'm leaving my friend Ice in charge of both while we're away."

"We could use some help to make repairs faster," Coal spoke.

"That's fine." He turned to Sky. "I'm returning to spend time with Mira. She's worried about this mission and I won't allow her to go. Do what you can here."

"Who is Mira?" Jill waited until Flint left her shuttle before asking.

Coal smiled at her. "He's in a family unit with a human woman."

"That's cool."

Chapter Eleven

Jill couldn't decide who looked more nervous as they assembled in the cargo hold of the *Jenny* to make the transfer to get the cyborg councilman back. They'd reached their meeting point with the smuggler crew. The *Cutter*, a shuttle larger than the *Jenny*, had just docked with them. The doors opened to allow the captain of the other shuttle to enter.

Flint met the man calmly. Jill could see how stunned the human guy seemed to be, surrounded by so many cyborgs, though there were only a handful of them. The captain appeared to be in his mid-to-late forties and as she watched, his expression changed. Rage contorted his features.

"Who owns this shuttle?"

The question startled Jill, along with everyone in the cargo hold. She stepped forward. "I do. I'm the one who asked David to hire you."

The captain of the other shuttle pointed his weapon straight at Jill. Fear gripped her but then movement from her left drew her attention from the dangerous adversary. Coal moved between them, putting his body in the path of the gun to shield her.

"Lower your gun," Flint ordered.

"My problem isn't with your men," the captain kept his voice calm. "Make that one move out of my way. I'm guessing you hired this shuttle to bring you here the way you hired me to bring your cyborg to you. That bitch is in possession of my property."

"Coal, stand down," Flint ordered. "It's a human issue."

Coal didn't budge. "No."

"That's an order he gave you, Coal." Onyx's voice grew cold. "We need the human male to get councilman Zorus back. He has him on his ship. She's irrelevant in comparison to our mission, according to the council. Stand aside."

Coal took a step back, his body bumping into Jill's, and his arm slipped behind his waist to curve around hers. He jerked her tighter against his body, holding her in place. "I'll protect her with my life."

Jill gripped his shirt, clinging to him, terrified he'd get shot pulling this stunt. She had no idea why the shuttle captain seemed intent on shooting her or what he thought she had that he owned.

"Coal?" She said his name softly. "It's okay. I don't want you to get hurt."

"You're going to die, you thieving bitch," the captain called out. "Although I plan to hurt you first to make you tell me who you obtained my shuttle from."

A frown marred her features and she bent sideways a little to peer at the enraged man. "Your shuttle? The *Jenny* is mine."

"Bullshit. It belonged to my partner and everything he owned became mine when he died."

He aimed at her face but Coal jerked her farther behind him to put her out of the line of fire. A deep growl came from the protective cyborg while his entire body turned rigid.

"Lower your weapon, Captain Varel," Flint ordered. "If you shoot him, I will have to kill you. What is the problem exactly?"

The captain hesitated. "This shuttle belongs to me and I want it back."

Confused, Jill tried to think of why the guy believed he had a right to the *Jenny*. She didn't stick her head out this time but instead kept still in Coal's embrace.

"Look, I don't know why you think it belongs to you but I inherited the *Jenny* from my father. I had nothing to do with it if he stole it from you. I honestly believed it belonged to him." She paused. "Let's talk about this, all right? Calmly."

"That sounds rational," Flint stated.

"Fine." The captain didn't sound happy but he agreed. "I'm holstering my weapon."

Coal relaxed and released her waist. Jill hesitated before inching over a little to peer at the captain while he put away his gun. Their gazes met and she didn't miss the pure fury radiating from his bright-green eyes, directed straight at her.

"This is my shuttle." A muscle along his jaw jumped. "Where did you get it from? I want names and locations. I want to track down whoever killed my partner."

"I'm not sure where my father got this but he had it docked to his ship. His men rebelled and I managed to escape on the *Jenny* before the *Viking* ended up being destroyed. I totally believed it belonged to him. That's all I know."

The captain's mouth dropped open and shock widened his eyes. "Jillian?"

It was Jill's turn to gape at him in surprise, her own mouth parting. "How do you know my name?"

The guy paled considerably. "My God. I didn't see it at first but you resemble your mother."

He took an uncertain step forward and then halted when Coal reached for his own weapon. The captain spread his hands open, away from his sides, clearly not going for his gun, but his attention remained fixed on Jill.

"I thought you died with Jim. I arrived a day too late and only found a debris field where his ship had been. He'd called me to meet up with him. We were silent partners and best friends since he first set out in space. I handled the Earth side of things while he traveled the outer regions of space. He became ill and told me he had only weeks to live, and wanted me to take care of you for him. It terrified him, thinking you'd be left alone."

Jill stood mute, trying to take in his words. This man knew her father? Her brain finally managed to form words. "Take care of me?"

He nodded. "With him gone, he wanted someone to watch out for you, to protect you." He took an uncertain step forward. "He planned to introduce us and he knew I'd treat you the way you deserved. He set up a marriage pact between you and me."

Coal snarled and jerked his weapon from the holster, aiming it directly at the other man's chest. "She's not yours."

"Marriage pact?" Jill gasped, stunned, but managed to reach over to grip Coal's arm. She didn't go for the one holding the gun but needed to hold onto him to keep her knees from collapsing.

The captain looked uneasy while he stared at the barrel of Coal's weapon but then his gaze flicked to Jill's. "Yes. He regretted giving you to Darren and had no idea that asshole would abuse you. He wanted you with a man he trusted without question, someone who'd never hurt you in any way. That's why he chose me."

Jill had no words. None.

"It's going to be fine," the captain swore softly. He gave her a soft smile. "I'm going to take care of you and keep you safe. I'm so damn glad I found you, Jillian. I've been told so much about you from your dad that I feel as though I already know you. Your aunt knew about the pact. Mary didn't tell you?"

"She died on the *Viking* right after dad's crew turned on us." Jill still couldn't believe what the man said. It had to be some kind of sick, cosmic joke, but then anger at her father set in. "He had no right to tell you I'd marry you."

"I promise I'll make you happy, sweetheart." The captain gave her a soft smile.

"She's not your sweetheart." Coal's voice deepened into a rough, harsh tone. "I'll kill you if you come any closer to her."

The captain's shocked gaze glanced between Jill and Coal, paling again. "Shit." He took a step back as his attention jerked back to Jill. "Call him off. You have nothing to fear from me." He cleared his throat. "Are you sleeping with that?"

"Him," Sky ground out. "We're not things. We're people."

The captain turned his head to shoot a frown at Sky. "Sorry." He faced Jill again. "It's fine with me if you allowed him to touch you. I'm not angry. You did whatever you had to do to survive. Nobody needs to tell me what a miracle it is that you're still alive."

Flint moved forward suddenly. "Can we have councilman Zorus now? You can resolve your issue with the female after he's been returned to us. We are ready to pay you."

Captain Varel hesitated. "On one condition."

Flint growled under his breath. "We already made a deal. We hired you for a price we intend to pay when you return him to us."

"I'll allow your man to come aboard after you transfer the payment if I can talk to Jillian alone."

"No," Coal snarled. The hand gripping the weapon tensed.

"Holster your weapon," Flint ordered. "Now, Coal. That's a direct order."

Jill rubbed Coal's arm. "It's okay." She frowned at the captain. "Why do you want to talk to me?"

"No," Coal snarled again but he put away the gun. "You aren't speaking with him without me present."

"And that's why I want to talk to her alone." Captain Varel turned his attention to Flint. "Her father and I were best friends for over thirty years. If she wants to stay with you then I'll accept that happily. I just need an assurance that's what she wants." The captain jerked his head in Coal's direction. "With him acting that way, you should understand my need to ask her questions without the fear of him intimidating her. I won't believe what she says with him ready to shoot me if he hears something he doesn't like."

Jill opened her mouth to tell him that was plain stupid and how Coal wouldn't do that but Flint spoke first.

"Do you believe he knew your father, Jill?"

Her gaze locked on the captain. He appeared about the right age as her father had been, perhaps a few years younger, but he knew she looked similar to her mother. She'd heard that from her aunt her entire life. The sisters had different coloring so the guy couldn't have just seen her aunt and assumed they resembled each other. Her aunt had been blonde with dark-green eyes while Jill's mother had strawberry-blonde, almost-red hair and bright-blue eyes. He also obviously knew about Darren's abuse and her aunt's name.

"He called you his pumpkin," the man said softly. "When you were born, your hair looked more orange than anything else."

"I believe him," Jill announced. "Only my father would have shared that story and only with someone he trusted. It's also just like my father to have tried to give me to another man in marriage. He always had an annoying way of thinking he knew what would be best for me no matter how misguided it turned out to be."

Flint hesitated. "You will not undock with the *Jenny* but I will allow you to speak to her privately after you return the councilman to us. Once he is safely aboard we'll send her to talk to you on your ship…alone."

"No!" Coal glared at Flint. "He could harm her."

184

"He knew her father, they were friends, and he seems reasonable. I understand the logic of him wishing to speak to her without us present to sway her answers." Flint took a deep breath. "He won't undock from us and it will alleviate any concerns he may have."

Jill realized Coal looked about ready to snap. Killing the captain who had possession of the cyborg would be bad. The crew would probably kill the cyborg in retaliation, attack the *Jenny*, and the captain had a much better ship than her shuttle. She stepped forward and turned to face Coal.

"He won't hurt me, Coal. I'll be fine. It's one short conversation and then I'll be right back." Her voice lowered. "I need you to trust me, calm down, and don't lose control, okay?"

She watched him take deep breaths, emotions battling across his handsome features, and it touched her how worried he obviously felt for her. She forced a smile and nodded at him.

He swallowed hard, his Adam's apple showing, and rage finally won dominance in his expression. "A short conversation and if you aren't back soon," his gaze lifted to narrow on the other shuttle's captain, his look turning ice cold and deadly, "I will come for you."

"Good enough." Relief had her relaxing. She nodded at Flint. "We have a deal."

Captain Varel backed up. "Transfer the payment and I'll have your man come aboard. I'll be waiting for Jillian on the other side of the docking sleeve. No harm will come to her. You have my word as a gentleman."

Jill resisted rolling her eyes. Her father never hung out with men of good standing or even decent people. She didn't think the guy posed a threat to her though. Big Jim wouldn't have trusted just anyone. She inched closer to Coal and faced the docking doors, curious to see what a cyborg councilman looked like.

"Payment is transferred," Onyx said softly. "Check your account."

The captain gaped. "How? You haven't gone near a terminal."

Flint sighed. "We don't need to. Please check your account. You'll find the payment transferred."

One of the captain's crew lifted a pad to enter commands to their bank. It only took a few seconds for him to get confirmation. "It's been paid in full. I signaled for them to transfer him."

"Your man is on his way." Captain Varel smiled at Jill. "I'll see you in a few minutes when you've had time to catch up with your friend, Jillian."

She didn't correct the guy who obviously thought she knew the councilman. She watched the crew of the other shuttle back out of the *Jenny's* cargo hold. The tension in the room seemed to grow stronger instead of lessoning. Flint turned to meet Jill's gaze.

"Zorus isn't friendly toward humans. Why don't you please go wait in the hallway?"

She shook her head. "I'm fine."

He frowned. "Fine. Stay far away from him." His gaze shifted to Coal. "Don't allow her to speak to the councilman. It will only make him irritated and you want that family unit request to be approved easily. He'll have a say in it now that he's back."

Jill held her tongue but a dozen questions filled her head. She glanced around the room, seeing a lot of tension. Sky walked toward the other door to meet the councilman and show him to his room. Jill had been asked to give up her room in order for the man to have privacy. She'd agreed since it seemed important. If she were going to live with cyborgs, she didn't want to start by pissing off some bigwig in Coal's world.

All of a sudden, a tall, black-haired cyborg strolled into her cargo hold. A human woman followed him, looking a bit stunned and perhaps frightened. Flint and the man spoke but Jill couldn't hear much at all. They kept their tones soft and with her all the way across the room with Coal mostly blocking her, only a few words were distinguishable.

"Why does it look as if they are going to deck each other?" she whispered softly to Coal.

He backed up, touching her, and lowered his tone. "Councilman Zorus isn't well liked. He's made enemies."

"Well, he is some big shot council guy. I've never met a politician yet that I liked but somebody has to do that job."

The new cyborg walked across the cargo hold, moving closer to them with the human woman in tow but instead of opening the door to the corridor to lead the couple to the captain's quarters, Sky suddenly blocked the door. The couple stopped. The woman looked irritated and yanked on the cyborg who gripped her. She jerked out of his hold.

"What did he mean about buying me?" The woman definitely didn't sound happy.

The black-haired councilman turned his gaze on her. "I had to buy you from the humans to obtain your release."

Coal tensed when it seemed the human and the council guy started to argue about how much he'd paid for her and she wanted to repay him. Jill's eyebrows rose. The council guy intimidated her but the woman stood up to him, though he towered over her. He looked mean, cold, and then he ignored her, asking which shuttle they were on. The woman grabbed the guy.

"Talk to me. How much do I owe you?"

Flint ignored her too, explaining to Councilman Zorus that the ship belonged to Jill and that she and Coal were a couple. He also explained why they'd needed the shuttle to get them closer to Earth and gave Zorus a message the council had asked Flint to relay. A bored expression remained on the other cyborg's features. He finally nodded.

"I want clothing and a secure com link to the council."

"Fine." Flint moved closer. "Who is she and what do you want done with her?"

"She belongs to me." The new cyborg stated. "She isn't your concern."

The tension level in the room jumped by leaps and bounds. Even Coal seemed to turn to stone. Jill didn't know why it alarmed everyone so much but she knew she didn't like someone saying they had bought and now owned another person as if that woman didn't have a say in the matter.

Sky suddenly moved. "Give her to me, Councilman Zorus. I've taken enough of your shit for you to owe me. I'll even buy her from you."

Their voices lowered too much for Jill to hear but she could see raw anger on Sky's features. They argued softly and then suddenly Sky lunged,

188

nearly slamming his chest against the councilman's. His words rang clear in the cargo hold.

"You're a sick bastard who gets off on killing humans. You even made a few of them believe you were their friend before you attacked. You're the one who demanded all humans be made nothing but property on our planet and you've tried to order every female killed who hooked up with one of us. I'm sorry you survived, if you want the truth. I'd have been happier if you'd died on Earth. I won't stand by and watch you turn on this female. You've killed your last damn human." He pushed Zorus hard. "I want ownership of her and I'll fight you for it."

The human woman backed up as the two men went at each other. Jill gasped, stunned at seeing two cyborgs exchanging punches. Coal spun, an arm gripping her waist, and she suddenly found herself pinned against the bulkhead with his body pressing her tightly against it. She had to wiggle a little but when she finally freed her head enough to peer around him, what she saw made her gasp.

The human woman had a weapon aimed at the cyborgs, a terrified expression on her features, and the councilman yelled out a warning for no one to fire. He threatened to kill anyone who shot the woman. The crazy guy then stepped directly into the path of her weapon, shielding her from the other weapons pointed at her, including Coal's, which he'd drawn, then twisted to take aim, keeping Jill pinned at the same time.

"Move out of the way. We don't have a clear shot." Flint ordered Zorus.

"Let her shoot him," Sky offered. "Just don't kill her. Aim for her shoulder so she'll survive. She's just scared."

The crazy new cyborg didn't move but instead spoke softly to the woman. Jill strained to hear the conversation but she was too far away. Whatever the cyborg said had the woman's hand wavering, the gun lowering slightly but not enough to avoid shooting him if he came at her. Jill pushed hard on Coal.

"Let me go. I can talk to her. She's scared and I don't blame her."

"Stay out of it," Coal whispered. "It's a dangerous situation. I don't want you hurt."

Frustration had her biting back a curse but sudden movement drew her attention. The woman had been distracted by something. It gave the councilman an opportunity to lunge. He tackled the smaller woman and both of them hit the floor. Jill saw the man tear the weapon from the woman's fingers and then yell out.

"Get a medic. Her head is bleeding."

Jill softly cursed before raising her voice to be heard. "Someone get Arm in here right now."

Coal released her from the wall. "He's a military android with medic training."

"I'm on it." Onyx closed his eyes.

"That's just weird how they don't need to turn on a com system or type or talk into an access panel to control everything on my ship."

Coal smiled. "I'm glad you think that since I'm unable to do it."

She rubbed against him, her gaze straying to the downed couple on the floor. The councilman hovered over the woman, looking downright terrifying in his obvious rage. The woman lay unmoving.

Flint approached. "I want to return to the *Star*." He lowered his gaze to Jill. "Go talk to Captain Varel. After you conclude your meeting with him, we will be on our way." He paused, his attention turning to the doors that opened to allow Arm to enter, carrying a medical kit. "Please hurry."

"I will." Jill smiled at Coal. "This won't take long."

* * * * *

Coal wanted to argue with Flint and Jill. The idea of her going alone onto the human shuttle didn't sit well with him. "It could be dangerous."

Jill took a deep breath. "It's going to be fine. This guy knew my dad. I know his friends aren't exactly the types you want to invite to dinner but he seemed concerned. I'll just tell him everything is great. It won't take long. Even slime balls have a sense of duty when it comes to looking out for the families of their friends."

Her words didn't set him at ease. "If you don't come back soon, I will come get you."

She grinned and her hand rubbed the front of his shirt over his belly. "I know you will." She winked. "I love you."

"I love you too." The fierce emotion gripped him. "I just want to protect you."

"It's going to be fine."

191

"Let her go," Flint ordered. "The longer you stall this, the longer we remain here."

With a pat, Jill released him. "Don't worry so much, Coal. I'll be back before you know it."

He fought every instinct to grab her when she turned away. He held still. Jill seemed to like some independence. Forcing her to remain on the *Jenny* would only cause problems.

"She will return soon," Flint reminded him, his attention turning to the scene unfolding with the human woman and Zorus. "I'm more concerned about that."

Coal nodded. "He really hates humans."

"I know. Him buying one will give me nightmares but we have no right to interfere."

Coal's gaze cut to the exterior cargo door when it opened. Jill walked off the *Jenny* without glancing back. His fingers curled into fists at his side.

"Take deep breaths and remain calm. I find that pacing helps." Flint shrugged. "I'll go see how the human female is." He looked at Onyx and Sky. "Guard the cargo door to make certain Coal doesn't get impatient. The last thing we need is a battle." He glanced around the cargo hold. "This thing wouldn't survive."

Coal shot Flint a glare. "I don't need babysitters."

"Yes, you do. I see that look, my friend. You want to storm after her to make sure she's fine. The captain won't harm her." Flint moved away.

Coal glared at the two cyborgs who moved to stand in front of the doors Jill had just walked through. He crossed his arms over his chest and began to pace. *She will return soon.* He kept repeating that in his mind.

* * * * *

Jill tried not to feel nervous as Captain Varel took total stock of her from head to toe, his green gaze slowly traveling the length of her body until he looked her in the eye again. He smiled.

"You can call me Barney," he offered softly. "I'm so glad to meet you finally, Jillian."

"Nobody calls me that. I'm just Jill." She shifted her stance. "Look, if my father said I'd marry you, well, he didn't have a right to do that." Her arms crossed over her chest. "It's not happening."

The calm expression on the captain's face quickly changed. "You don't know me. I believe, if given time, you will change your mind. I'd never treat you the way Darren did. You have nothing to fear from me."

"Let me cut the crap," Jill frowned back at him. "Did you see that tall, bald cyborg? I'm in love with him and he's the one I'm marrying. Nothing you could say or do will change that."

"You can't be serious."

The doors opened from the inner ship and a woman wearing barely anything walked into the cargo hold. She carried a tray with two glasses. Jill's eyebrows arched high at the tall, beautiful blonde woman with more leg bared than could be considered decent. The very short dress stretched over her thin, willowy frame, tight enough to reveal her small breasts to the point that nothing had been left to the imagination.

"Here are the drinks you ordered, Captain." The woman flashed a smile at Jill. "Welcome aboard."

"Thank you," the captain took the two glasses off the tray and dismissed the woman with a jerk of his head. He offered one of the drinks to Jill. "I bet you miss certain things from Earth. I thought you'd enjoy a glass of wine while we talked."

Jill watched the other woman stroll out of the room. "She's gorgeous." Her gaze returned to the captain. "You obviously don't need a woman in your life."

"She's a sex android for the crew."

"Oh." Shocked, she reached for the offered glass, in need of something to wet her dry throat. "Well, that's handy to have aboard. She looks so real I never would have guessed but then I've never seen one."

Barney grinned. "I don't use her for sex. We got a good deal on her that I couldn't resist. She was a decommissioned model heading to be scraped."

"That's hard to believe. She's lovely."

"They tried some sort of new thinking chip that made them too smart for whorehouses. We don't mind her adapting abilities since she's capable of learning everything from shuttle repairs to doing laundry."

"Handy." Jill sipped the wine again, enjoying the taste, and then lowered her glass. "Back to our discussion. I don't want to hurt your feelings but my life isn't going to be with you. It would never work out between us.

194

I really do love Coal. That's the name of the cyborg who wanted to shoot you." She paused. "My mind is made up."

"I see." He took a deep breath. "Do you mind telling me why you stayed away from Earth for so long? Have you been with those cyborgs since your father died?"

"Actually, I just met him and everything fell into place. I didn't come back to Earth because the *Jenny* didn't have enough fuel to make the trip. One of my first trades went wrong and a few people died accidentally when I tried to get away from a shuttle chasing me. I thought Earth Government wanted to arrest me for their deaths."

"You aren't wanted. I would have seen it if an alert had been issued on a Jillian Maris."

"It's a relief to know I'm not considered a murderer." She took another sip of the wine. "I'd like to go now."

He nodded. "At least finish your wine. I'm glad you're happy, Jillian. That's all your father wanted for you."

"I'm glad we're cool. You seem nice but as I said, I love Coal and I just want to get back to him." She lifted her glass, gulping down the rest of the wine just to be done, and held out the glass. "Thank you for being so understanding. I wish you a happy life."

He took the glass, smiled, and then tossed both glasses to the deck. His lunged before the sound of shattering glass registered to Jill. She gasped when he grabbed her, yanking her roughly against his larger frame.

"You didn't really think I'd allow you to get away, did you?"

195

Jill started to struggle but suddenly she didn't feel well. Her head started to pound, the room spun, and a dizzy spell hit her so hard her knees gave way. "What—"

"I drugged your drink, you naïve little fool." The captain shifted his hold and swept her up into the cradle of his arms. "Did you record all that?" His voice rose.

"Yes, Captain," a male answered from somewhere.

Jill fought to remain conscious. The pain in her head grew worse and when she tried to focus, she couldn't see anything but blurry shapes. Her arms and legs didn't want to respond.

"Loop it up and send the message. Tell them you'll only give it to that one called Flint. He seemed to command those robotic things. After you send it, undock, and get us the hell out of here before they realized they've been duped."

"No," Jill whispered. "Coal!" Everything turned black.

Chapter Twelve

Alarm gripped Coal when the engines to the *Jenny* fired up. He turned to the docking doors but they hadn't opened again to admit Jill back onto her ship. Onyx and Sky still blocked the doors but now both men gave him worried looks. Another door opened, drawing his attention, and he spun to face Flint.

"Why have you started the engines? Jill hasn't returned yet."

Flint walked straight to him, a frown fixed firmly on his face. "I have bad news, Coal." He stopped within feet between him. "Your human female decided to stay with her own people."

"I don't believe it. They are making her say that." He lunged, trying to get around the other cyborg toward the docking doors but Flint grabbed his arms, halting him.

"I've been given a message for you."

"Let me go. I'm going to retrieve Jill." Coal struggled but the other cyborg refused to release him.

"I'm going to play Jill's message for you." Flint cocked his head. "Listen."

The speakers in the docking back clicked on. Coal tensed, ceasing his struggles in the other male's arms. It had to be some kind of trick. The humans had stolen Jill. She loved him and would never leave him. They were going to form a family unit.

"Let me just be blunt, Coal." Jill's voice filled his ears. "I don't want to hurt your feelings but my life isn't going to be with you. My mind is made up. I just met him and everything fell into place. You seem nice but it would never work out between us. Thank you for being so understanding. I wish you a happy life."

The transmission cut out. Pain gripped Coal so hard he couldn't breathe. *No*, his mind screamed. *She wouldn't do this to me. She loves me and I love her.*

"I'm sorry," Flint whispered.

Coal shook his head, pushing past the pain in his chest. He glared at Flint. "It's a lie. Jill wouldn't wish to remain with them. She wants to join a family unit with me. It's some kind of trick. They used a voice modifier."

Sky had moved closer. "We all studied the message before we played it for you, man. That's her real voice. Modifiers take words and repeat them. There were many variations in her speech with common words to make it conclusive she actually said that."

Onyx gave him a sad look. "I am sorry, Coal. I agree with Sky. The message wasn't automated. She spoke the words."

Fury and disbelief boiled in Coal. "No." He suddenly pushed hard at Flint. "I do not believe it. Jill loves me and I love her. She wants me, not some human male. I am all she wants. They forced her to say those things. I'm getting my woman."

Flint managed to keep hold of him until Coal threw a punch. His fist slammed into the other cyborg hard, making direct contact with Flint's chin. The large cyborg grunted, his hold loosening, and then he stumbled.

Coal tore out of his grasp, running at the two stunned cyborgs still in his way. Onyx tensed, lifting and spreading his arms in an attempt to block him but Sky jumped out of the way. Coal hit Onyx in a tackle, taking them both down hard to the deck floor. Curses came from the pinned cyborg, his struggles weak from the trauma of having his body crash into the unforgiving metal and Coal's impressive weight crushing down on top of him. With one punch, Coal knocked the male under him unconscious. He rolled to get to his feet but pain exploded in the back of his head.

He collapsed on his side, nausea and strong waves of darkness nearly blinding him. Sky leaned down, holding something gripped in his hands.

"Sorry, my man. We've already undocked. You tear open that door and we're going to die. I thought you were a hell of a cute couple but you can't force her to stay with you."

Coal shook his head, pain making him groan. He blinked rapidly but his vision seemed to get worse instead of better. His hands pushed on the deck. He needed to find Jill.

"Stay down. I don't want to hit you again."

The strength in his arms gave way and he slumped to the deck. Jill needed him. She wouldn't leave him. They loved each other. *I love her*, he thought.

Flint bent over him. He sighed. "Lock him down before he wakes. I knew he'd take this hard."

I'm awake, Coal thought but his mouth didn't work.

"Who the fuck wouldn't? If I ever get a woman, I wouldn't want to let her go either." Sky sighed. "This bites ass."

199

Coal lost consciousness.

* * * * *

A warm, wet cloth gently brushed Jill's brow and she smiled. "Aunt Mary." Childhood memories flooded her and how her aunt had always done that when she had a fever. Her head did hurt a little.

"I am called Rune."

The soft, unfamiliar female voice had Jill struggling to open her eyes. She blinked, flinching from the light that momentarily blinded her, and then stared up at a lovely face of a blonde woman. She looked familiar but Jill couldn't place where she knew her from.

"How do you feel? I accessed the drug information you were given and it states side effects can cause headache, dry mouth, and dehydration."

Jill blinked, adjusting to the light, and fought to remember who the woman could be. She came up with a blank but then something tugged at her memory. It all came back so suddenly that she gasped. She tried to jerk upright but then groaned loudly when the pain in her head exploded into a throbbing mass of agony.

Gentle hands pushed her back down. "Easy. I have water for you to drink. Here. Sip."

A thin tube pressed against her lips and Jill drank. The cool water helped a lot, making her feel less like shit. Her eyes focused on the sex android. That deceitful bastard had drugged her. She tried to move her arms but then realized she only had restricted movement. She glanced down at the shackles on both wrists connected to something under the bed or perhaps to the floor. Her anger started to rise.

"Where is Captain Varel?"

Almond-shaped eyes shifted to the left. "Accessing the computer to locate Captain Varel." Her gaze fixed on Jill. "He's having a meeting with his crew in the conference room on the first level of the *Cutter.* You are on his shuttle."

"How long have I been out?"

The woman's eyes shifted left again and then back to Jill. "Two hours, six minutes, and fourteen seconds since I became aware of your drugging."

Jill lifted her hands. "Can you remove these?"

Rune nodded. "Yes."

"Will you please?"

"You will attempt to escape. That is what Captain Varel said when I asked him why he chained you."

"That's right. I need to get off this ship and back to my own before we undock."

"That has happened. The shuttle *Jenny* is no longer docked to the shuttle *Cutter.*"

Fear gripped Jill hard. "They blew it up?"

"No." Rune's eyes shifted left. "It flew away without incident and we travel toward the moon." Her gaze straightened out. "We are going to Captain Varel's home. It is pretty."

Jill clenched her teeth. "I need to get off this ship."

"Why?" Rune cocked her head.

"If I give you a direct order to remove these, will you do it?"

"I can cause no severe harm to living beings. There is a possibility of you being killed if I free you."

"If you don't let me go, I'm definitely going to be in a world of shit. Please?"

"Explain."

"You really are an android, aren't you?" Rune could pass for human easily in Jill's estimation and since the woman sat on the edge of the bed just feet from her, she couldn't have gotten a much closer inspection. "It's amazing how life-like you are."

"I'm an advanced model with enhancements. I am the most recent production of the sexual-aid android bots they created, state-of-the-art, and made of the finest genetic cloning research."

"Why did they decommission you then?" Jill wondered if the captain had lied about that. Maybe he'd stolen the android. She also needed to learn how to get the droid to help her.

"They gave me too much data capacity with sophisticated programming to adapt and learn."

"That doesn't sound bad."

Rune blinked. "I have been created to cater to the sexual urges of men but I refuse to allow them to use me in that capacity. It's illogical, messy, and I always can find better uses for my time."

Jill gaped.

Rune blinked again and then softly smiled. "Do you want more water? I could bring you food. I enjoy doing tasks as long as they don't involve men trying to touch me. I do not have real emotions or feelings but I have discovered the sensation of touch bores me." She kept her smile in place. "I enjoy chores. It keeps me occupied."

Okay, now I know why they dumped the plans for this model, she thought, smiling despite her circumstances at the irony of it. Rune had to be the most drop-dead beautiful woman she'd ever seen. The crew had to go crazy seeing her but not being able to use her.

"Will you please remove these?" Jill waved her shackled wrists. "I have to escape."

"I still don't understand why you wish to leave."

"I'm not marrying Captain Varel. He's going to be really angry when I refuse and probably kill me. I want to be long gone before he comes after me. I belong to someone else and I don't know why he hasn't come for me yet but he will. I'd like to get the hell out of here though, instead of waiting for Coal to catch up to me. Does the *Cutter* have life pods?"

"Affirmative." Rune reached for Jill's restraints. "Definite harm overrides a possibility." Her fingers gripped the metal. "I will crush them. Hold very still."

"Thank you." Gratitude had Jill breathing easier. She needed to get to a life pod, launch, and contact the *Jenny* to help them locate her. The image of Coal going crazy with worry had her silently urging the android to work faster.

The metal groaned and then snapped where the joints met. Rune eased the pressure instantly, pulling the broken shackles away. Jill climbed off the big bed, her gaze flashing quickly around the room, looking for a weapon in case she came in contact with someone.

"They took your shoes. They are not here and I do not know where they were taken."

Jill looked down at her bare feet, not realizing until that moment that she no longer wore her clothes but something that resembled silky, two-piece, short-sleeved pajamas with loose pants.

"I changed your clothing. Captain Varel hated what you wore and threatened to burn it on you."

"I'm really starting to hate that creep." She walked over to a table, picked up what passed for a sculpture of some sort, and gripped it. The smooth metal had a nice weight to it and parts of it were sharp at the top.

"That's abstract art of a fish with waves. It reminds Captain Varel of his fishing trips with his father as a boy."

Jill frowned at it. "I don't see it. To me it's a mess of twisted pointy metal with some curves to it and a lump of metal near the base."

"I do not see what he states is there but he said it is worth a lot of money."

"Now it's actually got a purpose." Jill walked to the door but it didn't automatically open as she approached. It brought her to a halt. "Is it locked?"

"Would you like me to open it?"

"Please." Jill turned her head and gave the android a grim look. "Could you show me where the life pods are?"

"Affirmative." Rune rose to her feet. "I must point out it is dangerous for you to use one. There's a fourteen percent chance of it being picked up by another ship. There is a sixty-two percent chance the *Cutter* will capture you. Your odds of safely reaching the *Jenny* are only twenty-two percent in your favor."

Jill did the math. "What about the missing two percent?"

Rune stopped next to Jill and the doors slid open. The android gave her a warm smile. "The pod could malfunction and blow up when you jettison away. Death would be instantaneous."

"Great." Jill wished the android hadn't shared that little possibility with her. "Lead the way please."

The droid turned left. "The pods are one level lower. We'll take the lift down."

"Thank you for this." Jill meant it. She just wanted to get away from her father's insane, woman-drugging friend.

"I enjoy being helpful."

"You really are."

They entered the lift. Rune didn't touch the buttons but the doors closed. "You can remote link to the computer?"

"Yes." Rune smiled. "It saves time while I move around the ship to do my chores."

Thoughts of Coal had Jill really edgy to get to the life pod. The things were designed to full blast away from ships in case of pirate takeovers or ship failures. As long as the *Jenny* hadn't gotten too far away she should be able to hail them to pick her up before the *Cutter* would have time to catch her.

What if Captain Varel comes after me? Her eyes closed with that thought. Her ship wouldn't be great in a shuttle-to-shuttle battle but then Coal had taken out a huge freighter. Her eyes opened when the lift doors did. She had faith he would think of something to save their asses again if it came down to it.

They stepped into a cargo hold. Two life pods were secured to the deck near the far bulkhead by the exterior loading doors. Jill jogged forward, intent on releasing one of them from the tethers. All she'd have to do would be to activate the docking doors, seal the pod, and it would get sucked out. She would activate the engines at that point to get her away from the *Cutter*.

"What are you doing, Rune?"

The male voice made Jill spin toward another door she hadn't seen. Captain Varel stood there glaring at the android. Four of his men were behind him, looking mean, unhappy, and tough.

"Are you giving our guest a tour?" Sarcasm dripped from Barney Varel's cold tone.

"She doesn't wish to marry you." Rune shrugged. "She made logical arguments to release her."

"You stupid, useless pile of synthetic skin." The captain jerked his head. "I should have allowed that driver to take you to the incinerator factory instead of trading a barrel of banned booze for you." His cold stare landed on Jill. "Where do you think you were going?"

Fear made Jill's heart race. "You can't force me to marry you. Coal will come after me."

He grinned coldly. "That dumb hulk of silver skin? He believes you met me and fell madly in love." His boots struck the deck when he approached. "I'm irresistible."

Her gaze darted frantically around the cargo hold, looking for an escape, but there wasn't one. She backed up as he and his men approached. They spread out to corral her into a corner.

"Why are you doing this? I thought you said you were friends with my father. Big Jim obviously trusted you."

The captain paused, holding up a hand to stop his advancing men. "Let me tell you about your daddy, Jillian. We had a twenty-eighty profit split. Want to guess who got the much lower portion?" His face turned red. "Me. He ended up richer than I could ever dream of being while I still have to work just to keep paying for my lifestyle. He promised me he'd leave me something but do you know what he did instead?"

Jill's shoulders straightened and some of her fear eased to a cold kind of anger. "Let me guess. He screwed you over somehow. I thought you said you knew him. He had a reputation for being a total bastard. Didn't that 'bloody' part of his nickname tip you off that he wasn't the nicest guy?"

"He left me you," Barney Varel snarled.

"Then problem solved. I'll be out of your hair forever. I don't care if you promised to take care of me. I swear you'll never see me again if you just let me go."

The smile he gave Jill froze her inside. She'd never seen so much animosity directed at her. "You don't understand. Jim happened to be the most ruthless yet intelligent man I ever met. He wanted to make certain I kept you alive and well after he died. He left you all the money he had."

Jill blinked repeatedly, staring at the man blankly. "I don't have his money. If it was on his ship, it went with him when *Viking* blew up. The *Jenny* and the cargo aboard it were all I inherited."

"You don't understand."

"You're right. I don't."

Jill backed up until the bulkhead trapped her with nowhere else to go when he inched closer. Captain Varel glared down at her from his slightly taller height and lifted a hand. His finger pointed directly at her chest, pressing right over her left breast.

"You're the key to his money."

Jill pushed against his chest with both hands, hard enough to knock him back a few stumbling steps. "He never said a word to me about where his money is. Do you think if I knew where it was that I'd be trading with lowlifes in deep space, risking my neck on every job? I can't even afford to pay a crew. I work with three androids I salvaged. I love the *Jenny* but that shuttle has more things broken down on it than what actually works."

"Unbelievable. He seriously never told you?" Disbelief widened the guy's eyes.

"No."

The scowl returned. "Have you ever heard of a three-scan lock bank?"

"No."

"Your father had. There are two of them on Earth. That's where all his money is stored."

Jill was not sure what to say.

"Damn stupid bitch," he hissed. "They use scans to access the account information. Instead of numbers or passwords or even identification cards, they use your DNA from a blood sample, a genetic scan of your hair, and a retinal scan of your eye."

Confused, Jill just gawked at him.

"You're coded into the account."

Realization slowly dawned. "You mean—"

He cut her off. "To access it, you have to be alive. Dead or frozen blood is detected, rejected, and it won't allow access. The same goes for your hair and retinal scans. It verifies you're alive every damn time. Your father set up the account with a cap on how much can be withdrawn any given time." He stepped closer but then halted, his hands gripping his hips so hard that his knuckles turned white. "It's going to take me at least ten years of keeping you alive to use you to withdraw all of it."

Horror gripped Jill. "You can have it all. I don't want it. I just want you to let me go."

"Never," he ground out harshly. "At least not for the next ten years, sweetheart. After the account is drained I don't give a damn what happens to you."

This can't be happening, she thought.

"Jim felt certain I'd fall in love and grow to care for you in that time." The captain snorted. "Not damn likely but I will make a deal with you."

Jill met his cold glare, feeling numb inside.

"I won't beat the shit out of you every time you pull this kind of stunt if you behave and stop trying to escape. If you're really good, I may even allow you to walk away from me at the end still breathing."

Tears blinded her but she tried to blink them back. "Coal will come for me." *God, I hope so. Please*, she silently pleaded.

"The cyborg?" Captain Varel turned his head, grinned at his men, and darted an amused look at each one of them. The amusement left his expression. "She thinks metal heads are intelligent." He suddenly lunged, a hand fisting in Jill's hair.

She cried out when he jerked her away from the bulkhead, spun her to face away from him, and his other arm wrapped around her waist. He held her in front of him. She didn't fight. The pain of her hair being pulled by the tight grip he had on her kept her still.

"Watch how damn smart they are," he whispered in her ear, his hot breath making her nauseous from the unwanted intimacy of his body pressed so close to hers.

His crew chuckled and some outright laughed. Varel took a deep breath before speaking.

"Rune? Clean the damn deck. It's dirty."

The android smiled. "Of course." She turned and walked to a cabinet, opened it, and removed foam-cleanser canisters.

"She refuses to have sex with the men, will fight them off if they try to touch her, but they don't need to," he whispered.

Rune reached for the hem of her short dress, gripped it, and pulled it over her head. She placed her dress on a hook inside the cabinet and then turned, totally naked, to face them. Jill's gaze traveled down the android's perfectly formed naked body. Rune started to spray down a section of the deck, grabbed a handful of towels, and then dropped to her hands and knees. She started to scrub the deck.

"She doesn't want to get her clothes dirty. See how smart she is? She refuses to be a sex aid to men but she's too stupid to know we get off on her all the time." Varel jerked on Jill's hair, forcing her head to turn. "See how easy it is to fool them? Your metal head believes what he's told. Right now he thinks you're happy with the man you were meant to be with. He's never coming for you."

One of the crew opened his pants, revealing that he didn't wear underwear and that the sight of the anatomically correct android turned him on. His hand squeezed his stiff cock, slowly pumping his fist around it while he watched Rune on her hands and knees, moving back and forth.

"I'm going to puke," Jill whispered, squeezing her eyes closed as another man unfastened his pants.

"Go ahead," Varel laughed. "Rune will just spend more time wiggling that perfect, upturned ass for the men to jack-off to. She does have a habit of spreading her knees to really scrub hard." He suddenly moved, yanking Jill toward the door. "If you try to escape again, I will beat you. I just have to keep you alive, hair on your head for the scans, and make sure nothing happens to those pretty blue eyes of yours. Scans don't give a shit if you're in pain or bruised up."

Chapter Thirteen

Coal woke with a vengeance. Rage and the pain from the blow to the back of his head had him snarling. Sky had hit him with something, knocked him out, and the *Cutter* had more time to take Jill farther away from him. His muscles against the chains holding him to the same cargo table he'd been bound to when he'd first entered the *Jenny*.

"You will be fine," Arm stated.

Coal's head twisted to the side, spotting the android near the corner, and tried to push his mind to work through the foggy ache he experienced. "Come here."

Arm came forward and stopped at the side of the table. With shrewd eyes, Coal stared up at the damaged face of Jill's military droid.

"Do I still have access to you?"

"Yes, Sir."

"Release me now."

"I have been ordered not to do that unless there was a medical reason."

"My right arm hurts. I need to move it to alleviate the pain. I can't do that chained down."

Arm suddenly reached out, his strong fingers gripping the metal above Coal's wrist, and snapped the links. Coal wanted to yell out in victory but managed to remain calm. He needed to act quickly before one of his cyborg brothers decided to check on him. Jill had been smarter by ordering the

213

droid not to release him under any circumstance unless she'd given Arm a direct order. Of course, it helped that the defense model had outdated systems. A newer model would have never fallen for that ruse.

"My other arm and both legs need movement. I have cramps in them that hurt me severely," he lied.

Arm freed him quickly. Coal stood and ordered Arm to turn around. The big droid spun to present Coal with its back. In seconds Coal opened his access panel. He disconnected the device that allowed data to be transmitted to the android without a direct connection to a terminal.

"Why have you shut down my receptors? Were they malfunctioning?"

"Yes." Coal blew out a deep breath, relieved he had total control of Arm for the time being. "You were being hacked. Now it isn't possible for someone to send you orders. You're to only do what I tell you from now on. Disregard everyone else."

"Understood."

Coal closed the panel and headed for the weapons locker. "I need your help."

"Understood." Arm followed him. "What are my orders, Sir?"

"Is there a safeguard in case the shuttle is overtaken to regain control?"

Arm paused. "No, Sir."

Frustration gripped Coal as he strapped on weapons. He needed to regain control of the *Jenny*. "You're a defense droid. Are you skilled with non-lethal tactics to take out humans without causing permanent injury?"

214

"Affirmative."

Coal turned, staring at the droid's damaged face. "What is the quickest way to do that, causing the least injury?"

A mechanical whine sounded and part of Arm's side slid open. "I am equipped with hostage bombs."

"What are those?" Coal peered at the round green balls displayed in casing, in a row.

"Avarios gas, Sir."

"I don't know what that is." Coal frowned.

"They explode on impact, the non-lethal gas fills a square radius of fifty feet, and once breathed in by life forms it makes them lose consciousness within seconds, Sir. The effects are harmless with only a ten percent chance of slight to severe injury caused by falls when they collapse from the affects of being subjected to the gas."

"Do you carry any masks to prevent me from being effected or know of any onboard?"

"No, Sir."

"How long does it take the gas to dissipate?"

"One minute and nine seconds, Sir."

Coal took a deep breath, held it, and walked to the terminal that was located inside the door of the cargo hold that led inside the shuttle. He activated the onboard computer, guessing he didn't have much time before someone noticed the breach. He read life signs on the shuttle. He turned, pulling air into his starving lungs, and knew how long he could hold his breath.

"There are two life forms in the mess hall and one in cabin three. Go locate them. When you find them I want you to toss one avarios-gas ball, wait one minute, then toss a second one. Keep them pinned down until they fall over. Are my orders clear?"

"Yes, Sir." Arm paused. "There are six life forms aboard, including you, at my last scan. I cannot verify that number now that my receptors have malfunctioned."

"Ignore the two sealed in the captain's quarters. The councilman and the human are highly unlikely to leave that section of the ship, but if they do, gas them as well. Under no circumstances are you to kill anyone. Repeat the order."

"Use only non-lethal gas to contain the life form threats."

"Go. Return to me when it's done."

"Yes, Sir." Arm spun around, moving fast for the doors.

Coal closed his eyes. He had no idea what the consequences of his actions for ordering the droid to attack fellow cyborgs would be, but whatever they were, he'd face it after he had Jill back in his arms. Grim determination stilled his inner turmoil over disobeying orders. He'd die for Jill.

* * * * *

Jill kicked out at Barney Varel, her bare foot impacting with his thigh, and pain shot through her toes. Without boots on it hurt when she nailed him. The man grunted but didn't release her arm.

"Knock it off, you little hellion. You look like your mother but you act just like your father."

"Let me go," she twisted hard, attempting to free her wrist from the bruising grip he had on her.

"Put your damn thumb on the scanner."

"You already tore a handful of my hair out, you bastard!"

"It was just a few strands. The bank is waiting for the second verification." His hold tightened, drawing a cry of pain from her, and forced the electronic pad closer. "Do it or I swear I'll knock out some of your teeth. I want access to that account."

"Fine." She ceased her struggles, jammed her thumb down on the pad, and winced when the needle pierced her skin to draw blood to take a DNA sample.

The scanner beeped to verify her identity. The captain released her wrist and lunged for her when she tried to spin away to put distance between them. His fingers dug into her hair at the base of her neck, fisting a handful of it, and shoved the scanner in front of her face. Her back ended up pressed against his torso.

"Look into the damn thing and don't you dare blink. I'm really getting pissed off at you."

"Screw you."

"If you don't stop fighting me, you will not enjoy the consequences. Remember your dear ex-husband? Your father told me what he did to you. Want a repeat?"

Jill went utterly still. He didn't say it but he implied he'd rape her. Her eyes widened and she looked at the center of the pad, not blinking. She didn't care about her father's money but she hated Varel enough to try to take a stand against him getting a single credit though it wasn't worth him hurting her that severely.

A red light blinded her for an instant and then the pad beeped again. Varel laughed, giving her a vicious push forward. Jill stumbled, nearly collapsed to her knees, but managed to stay on her feet. She walked to the other side of the quarters, as far as she could get from the vile man. Once there she glared at him, put her back to the wall, and tensed to attack him if he came at her.

Varel's full attention remained on the electric pad while he punched in commands. He grinned widely and looked super pleased at whatever the device displayed.

"Sweetheart, you've made me a happy man."

"You got what you wanted. Please leave."

"Don't you enjoy my company?"

Jill rubbed her throbbing thumb. "No."

"Do you know what I'm going to call you?" He didn't wait for a response. "My bitchy little banker."

Jill held her tongue. The guy had gone from anger to being annoyingly happy now that he'd gotten what he wanted from her. She didn't want to anger him again. She just wanted him to leave her alone in the room.

"Want to celebrate with me?" His grin widened and his gaze lowered to her chest. "I always wanted to fuck your mother but Jim would have killed me for touching something of his."

Heart pounding, Jill fought fear and nausea at the idea of him wanting to have sex with her. "You're a sick, perverted psycho."

His blond eyebrows shot up. "Me?" He gave her a cold look. "At least I didn't let one of those metal heads screw me. That's perverted. He's not even attractive. I don't know how you allowed it to touch you."

"Coal isn't a metal head. He's twice the man you are."

"Built them with big dicks, did they? Wait until you see mine. You won't be disappointed."

"I meant he's not a lowlife scum." She paused. "I know you're a big dick already and if you open those pants, I'll try to rip it off."

"You better start learning to be nice to me. We're going to be together for a very long time."

"Coal is going to come for me."

"That stupid metal head thinks you dumped him. Right now he's probably two solar systems away and happy to be rid of you."

The doors opened and Captain Varel cursed, curling his lip at Rune.

"I brought food for Jillian." She walked toward a table with the tray she held.

"Get out," Varel ordered her. "I didn't tell you to do that."

Rune ignored him, placing the food down, and pulled out a chair. "Sit, Jillian. It's warm. You should eat it soon before it cools." She calmly stared at the captain. "If you persist to harass Jillian I will escort you out of the room to rethink your ill-advised plan."

"Goddamn androids. I'm going to dump you in open space, Rune. Do you hear me, you useless pile of synthetic skin?"

Rune waved to the chair. "Sit, Jillian."

"Fuck!" Varel spun and stormed out of the room.

Jill relaxed. "You have good timing. Thank you."

"Timing had nothing to do with my bringing you food. I monitored the room and noticed your accelerated heart rate, indicating fear. I also listened to Captain Varel's conversation with you by accessing the coms. You don't want your body spoiled with male fluids. You aren't strong enough to stop any attempts males make to use your body, the way I have been designed. No one should be forced to endure boredom. I may not harm humans but nowhere in my programming does it state I am unable to physically move them to another location. When the males have attempted to touch my body I have secured them in cabinets in the cargo hold."

"You what?"

"I lock them in cabinets. Eventually I release them before they suffocate if another crew member doesn't find them. Harming a human is against my programming. Please eat before your food cools. I have been told it tastes better heated."

"I think I adore you."

Rune cocked her head. "Adore? I don't understand why you would feel that emotion where I am concerned."

"If we get out of this, do you want to come with me? I have three androids on my ship. No one would try to touch you."

"I am the property of Captain Barney Varel."

"He illegally traded to get you."

Rune's gaze drifted to the left, something Jill realized the android did when she processed information. "An illegal transaction is null and void."

"Exactly," Jill agreed, sat down, and started to eat. "You don't belong to that asshole."

"I will leave with you until a proper owner for me has been established."

"You're free, Rune. No one owns you."

"You wish to own me?"

Jill hesitated. "I consider the androids on my ship friends. They are free too."

Rune's gaze drifted to the left and stayed there while Jill finished her meal. The android focused on Jill finally.

"The probability of you leaving the *Cutter* and obtaining permission from Captain Varel to take me with you is not in your favor."

"I'm not going to ask him if I can take you. I'm asking you. You're programmed to make decisions, right?"

"Affirmative. I take facts, process them, and decide accordingly."

"You—"

221

"Hold." Rune's eyes drifted left and she frowned. "Incoming shuttle approaching. Processing specifications." She paused. "They are ignoring hails." She paused again.

Jill's heart raced. "Could it be my ship? Is it the *Jenny*?"

"They used the moon to come closer to hide their signal before the sensors picked them up."

"Is it the *Jenny*, Rune? Answer me." Jill rose to her trembling legs. *Please let it be Coal*, she silently prayed.

Rune snapped out of her trance-like state. "Visual confirmed. Brace, Jill. The *Jenny* has just opened fire on the *Cutter*."

Joy seized Jill and she made a fist, pumping air. "YES!"

A loud noise filled the room, followed by rapid repeats of the same sound. The lighting flickered, the gravity stabilizers cut out, and Jill's feet left the floor as the emergency lights turned the room an eerie pale yellow as power failed. The weightless sensation had her crying out in fear, her arms and legs flailing. She tried to grab something and then the room around her violently moved. Jill hit the wall hard, bounced off, and realized she hadn't moved, it had.

A hand gripped Jill's upper arm, tugging at her floating body, and she turned her head. Rune had grabbed hold of a bulkhead beam to keep them from being batted around the room while keeping hold of Jill to tether her there as well.

"The computer is down," Rune stated, a baffled look on her face. "I'm unable to get any readings."

"We need to get to the cargo hold now. Coal will try to force dock to get to me."

"All power is out. I have no way to open the doors or locate the whereabouts of the crew to avoid them if we attempt to escape to the cargo hold."

"You're strong, right? Can't you force the door open?"

"You are correct. I'm able to do that." Rune pulled Jill closer to the bulkhead beam. "Hold on."

Jill had to move slowly without gravity, but she managed to get a good grasp on the metal. She watched Rune turn her body slightly, push one hand against the wall, and propel her body toward the door. The android moved gracefully as she floated down the wall to the door as if she did it every day.

"I can do that," Jill muttered, knowing she needed to reach the door when Rune got it open. She mimicked the move but when she pushed against the wall, releasing her grip on the beam, her body started to twist in circles as she floated.

"Damn it!" She fought dizziness after a few spins. "It looked easy."

* * * * *

"Ready?" Coal gripped the weapon. "If any humans attempt to breach the *Jenny* from that shuttle I want you to use lethal force unless it's Jill. You remember her, don't you?"

"Affirmative, Sir. Lethal force unless it is Jill."

"Kill those assholes if you see them. I plan to."

223

Anger propelled Coal forward with a determined purpose. He unlocked the door to the docking sleeve and stormed through it to the other ship. He had to shoot out the lock pad to destroy it and reach a hand inside to find the safety release. He got the door to the *Cutter* open.

He took a step inside only to discover he had an unforeseen problem. He'd knocked out their engines but he'd also managed to make them lose power. A growl tore from his throat as he realized he needed gravity boots to move about the ship faster to search for Jill. He turned, moving quickly, and entered the cargo hold of the *Jenny* again.

The doors to the interior opened, startling Coal, and his weapon rose instantly, training on the other male's chest. He stared at Sky. The cyborg froze upon spotting Coal. Sky blinked, staring back at him.

"You should be unconscious."

Sky hesitated. "I enjoy swimming on Garden. Working for Councilman Zorus pisses me off and the only thing that cools my temper is icy water with vigorous exercise. I can hold my breath for a very long time. I fooled the android into believing the gas put me to sleep." Sky swallowed. "What are we doing?"

"I attacked the *Cutter* and I'm going after Jill." Coal didn't look away from the other male. "Arm? Do you have more avarios-gas balls? Sky is willing to take some deep breaths now so I may complete my mission." His voice became threatening. "He has that option or being shot."

"Affirmative, Sir." Arm turned toward them.

"You could knock me out but wouldn't you like some help?" Sky smiled. "Everyone is unconscious except Zorus and the human but I see you

224

fused their door sealed. You also took the computer offline to prevent him from taking control of it." He paused. "No one is going to know if I help you get your girlfriend back."

Suspicion narrowed Coal's gaze. "Why would you do that?"

"Why the hell not?" Sky chuckled. "Besides, I like Jill. She's cool. You two are cute together. I'm all for getting her back for you but this time don't lose her again."

"It's not logical for you to risk punishment if you're caught helping me."

"Logic is overrated and I'm already in deep shit with Zorus over trying to warn the human he bought about what a prick he is. He said when I get to Garden he's going to make me sorry for interfering. You want my help or not?"

Coal took a deep breath, lowering his weapon. "We need gravity boots. They have no power."

Sky strolled into the room, still grinning. "Awesome."

Shaking his head, Coal moved to the cabinet that contained them. "You're a unique cyborg."

"I could say the same thing and I like that about you. Now let's go get your woman. I suggest using some handcuffs to keep her in your bed when you get her back. Women tend to find trouble when you let them out of one."

Coal stared wide-eyed at the other male. Sky shrugged and accepted the gravity boots handed to him.

"What? I'm the expert on all things human. Take my word, my man. Chain her to your bed and keep her there. She won't protest too much if you keep her happy while she's in it."

* * * * *

Jill slammed into another wall, wincing as her shoulder took the hit the hardest. Rune turned her head.

"If you would just do as I do, you would glide instead of bumping into things."

"I don't have your coordination."

"That is true. I will guide you."

Rune reached back, grabbed a handful of Jill's shirt, and then used her other hand to push off from the wall. They floated down the hallway in a straight line.

"I feel stupid," Jill muttered. "I should have asked you to do this when we left the room."

"We are almost there."

A scream suddenly pierced air. It gave Jill chills as the terrified sound cut out. Her heart pounded hard and Rune slowed their momentum by releasing Jill to open her arms, brushing the walls with her outstretched fingers. Jill bumped into her back but used her hands to cushion the impact.

"That was a male," Rune stated.

"Human?"

"Do cyborgs scream?"

Jill bit her lip. "I don't know. Maybe."

"I could access a door to remove us from a traveled corridor."

"No." Jill forced air into her lungs, trying to push down her fear. "We want to find the reason for the scream and I'm hoping its Coal."

A whining noise nearly deafened Jill and lights blinded her as the power came back on. The gravity stabilizers also came back but someone had adjusted them to return slowly. Jill saw the deck coming closer to her and released Rune, happy she wasn't turned head down as her feet brushed the floor and then her knees.

The return of gravity had her fighting not to throw up. Her sluggish body seemed to suddenly weigh a ton. She lay on the floor where she'd landed. Rune didn't seem to suffer any of the effects since she stood up quickly.

"Are you going to take a nap? This isn't a good time to do that. You are in danger."

Jill bit back a curse. "Really? I thought I'd just close my eyes for a few minutes."

"That wouldn't be wise."

"It's called sarcasm, Rune. Learn the definition of that word sometime. I'm trying to lift myself up but I have to readjust to the gravity." Sweat broke out on Jill's forehead as she pushed up with her arms. "Could you help me?"

Rune bent and gripped Jill to pull her to her unsteady feet. "Follow me. While I can't severely harm humans I can push one back if one attempts to attack you."

"That would be great." Jill lifted her leg and took a lurching step. "I think they overcompensated on the gravity."

Rune's eyes shifted left.

"You don't have to check."

Weapons fire came from somewhere near them. "Gravity is unstable." Rune met Jill's annoyed gaze. "I'm missing one crew member's life reading but two new ones have entered the *Cutter*. They are one corridor over, heading this way. Should we avoid them?"

"No!" Tears filled Jill's eyes. "It's got to be Coal."

"This makes you feel sadness that he has boarded the *Cutter*?"

"No. These are happy tears. Just find the new life readings."

"This way." Rune spun around. "Follow me."

Joy and excitement spurred Jill on. Weapons fire sounded again, someone yelled a curse, and then they were turning a corner. Rune suddenly stopped, her arms jerking out to the sides, and she blocked Jill from walking.

"I have a visual on two cyborgs and one crew member."

Jill moved, going on tiptoe, and stared over Rune's arm. One of the crew ran toward them but someone bigger tackled him, taking him down just feet from them. Coal landed on the man's back, a knife flashing in the air as it raised and then he buried it deep in the back of the man's neck. The guy screamed but with a vicious twist of his wrist, Coal ended the guy's life. His head lifted and his dark, furious gaze met hers.

"Jill!" He pushed up, got to his feet, and tore the blade out of the body in the same motion. He wiped the bloody blade on his pants and stormed toward her.

Rune released the wall and shoved Coal hard, sending him flying back to prevent him from reaching Jill.

"No!" Jill yelled and then launched herself around Rune to reach Coal.

He grunted when he landed on the deck on his ass but his arms lifted when she threw her body at his. He dropped the knife when she slammed into him, both of them falling flat, and Jill grinned.

"You came for me."

Coal's eyebrow arched as he wrapped his arms around her where she lay sprawled on top of his body.

"I am the right man for you, not the human male."

"Yes, you are." Jill grabbed his face and planted a kiss on his beautiful mouth.

Chapter Fourteen

"It appears she changed her mind about wanting to end your relationship," Sky stated calmly.

Jill tore her mouth away from Coal's and she gaped at the other cyborg standing with his feet braced apart by their heads, hovering there looking dangerous but amused. He gripped a large rifle-type weapon in the cradle of his arms while he smiled at her.

"I never wanted to leave Coal."

"That's not what your message stated." Sky shrugged. "I hear women do change their minds frequently but not all of my information is accurate."

"I didn't send Coal any message. That jerk drugged me and used the conversation I had with him to use my voice to mix one together."

"That's true," Rune confirmed. "It's a common practice Captain Varel and his men use to con potential victims to gain access to their banking accounts. They prod someone into a conversation then manipulate their words until they have enough sentence structures to fit their purpose. Most computer verifying voice programs are fooled but some are not."

"Hello, gorgeous." Sky cleared his throat. "Where have you been all my life?"

"Tell me how long you have been alive and I can give you a detailed account of my locations." Rune smiled at him warmly.

"She's an android named Rune," Jill warned softly. "She hates to be touched so don't hit on her."

Sky's grin died and his pale eyes seemed to glow. "No. Life can't be that cruel." His gaze ran the length of the leggy android and then softly cursed. "Now I finally get that old Earth saying— 'if it looks too good to be true then it probably is'. She's perfect."

"I have flaws," Rune kept her smile in place.

"Not from where I'm standing." Sky suddenly released the weapon handle to brush his palm quickly down the front of his leather pants while he adjusted his stance, obviously in some discomfort. "Down, boy."

Rune followed his hand with her gaze. "You have something alive in your pants?"

"Not for long." Sky's features hardened. "Sometimes it's good to be able to go numb in certain places when I set my mind to ignore shit."

Coal recovered from his shock of being knocked down, his body turning them until he rolled on top, and pinned Jill to the deck under him. His beautiful gaze searched hers. "I didn't care if you sent that message or not. It was irrelevant. You said yes after I gave you time to make certain you wanted to join a family unit with me. I'm holding you to it."

Jill's fingers trembled as she caressed his jawline, happy beyond words that he'd really come for her. "I love you, Coal."

"This isn't the time for the lovey-dovey crap," Sky reminded them gently. "I've hacked their system and we have company coming."

Coal braced his hands on the deck, pushed up, and straightened. He leaned down to offer her his hand. She gripped it tightly and he effortlessly pulled her to her feet.

"How close?" Coal bent to retrieve his knife, shoved it into the holder strapped to his hip, and rage hardened his features.

"Too damn close." Sky gripped his weapon again with both hands. "Rune? Is that your name? You need to move. You're blocking my shot."

Coal didn't move or release Jill. His gaze locked with hers. "Did he harm you? Did he touch you?"

Jill's mouth opened but Rune spoke first.

"He tried to soil her with his sexual fluids and frightened her but I interrupted before he could force use of her body. She isn't strong enough to have stopped him."

"Oh shit," Jill muttered, seeing a murderous look enter Coal's gaze.

He lifted his head to look at Sky. "The captain is mine."

"Good. Turn around then because he and four crew members are about to find us." Sky jerked his head toward where Rune stood. "They are closing fast."

The second Coal released her hand, spun, and planted his big body in front of her, Jill knew with certainty that Captain Barney Varel would be dead if Coal got his way. She waved frantically at Rune.

"Come on."

"Return to the *Jenny* now," Coal ordered.

Rune walked casually toward them as if she weren't aware of the danger they were in. Jill nearly envied the android. Fear inched up her spine for Coal's safety. "Let's just go. The docking door is right there. You've damaged the *Cutter* badly enough that I doubt it can give chase."

"Go to the *Jenny* now." Coal's tone sounded unusually harsh.

He's going to kill them all, Jill thought, backing away. If Captain Varel survived, he'd come after her. She knew that deep down. Her father had meant to protect her but instead he'd unknowingly made her a target for anyone who learned about his money when he'd made Jill the only key to access it.

She paused at the docking door, watching as Coal and Sky separated, getting behind crates piled by the doorway to the interior area of the ship. They both looked ready for battle with their weapons pointed in that direction. Jill hesitated and then inched toward the life pod to hunker down behind it.

"What are we doing?" Rune stood next to her, watching her with a curious look fixed on her features.

Jill reached up and gripped the android's hand at her side. "Crouch down. We're hiding. I'm not leaving Coal behind," she whispered. "Lower your voice too."

Rune hesitated before lowering to her knees. "Why?" She whispered back.

"I love him and if he gets into trouble, I'm going to try to save him."

Rune frowned. "You have no weapons."

"It doesn't matter. I can't wait for him in my ship just praying and pacing until he returns to me in one piece."

"I don't understand the logic in—"

"Silence," Jill hissed as the doors to the interior of the shuttle slid open.

One of the crew inched into the cargo hold gripping a portable laser cannon. Terror struck Jill when she saw it. One of those could literally cut a person in half with just one zap. Sky suddenly moved, lifted his own weapon, and fired. He aimed with deadly accuracy. The man screamed when his chest opened up.

Blood poured down the man's body. His distress lowered to a soft whimper before he fell over. The laser cannon skidded a few feet across the deck. Bile rose in Jill's throat at the gruesome sight but she fought it down, peeking around the nose of the life pod. She tried to ignore the guy's blood slowly spreading on the deck as it drained out of the dying man.

The doors remained open. The silence in the room became stifling to Jill as she waited to see what would happen next.

"I just want Jillian," Captain Varel yelled out. "You can have the shuttle without a fight. Let's make a deal."

The enraged growl that came from Coal reached Jill's ears, though it wasn't that loud. His voice rose when he spoke. "I will never allow you to have her but I will allow you a choice in how you die."

Silence stretched again. "I'll buy her from you," Varel offered. "Name your price."

"You can fight in a hand-to-hand battle with me or with weapons," Coal countered. "Your choice." He paused. "We have an armored military droid that I will send in after you."

"Take Jillian then and just get off my shuttle." Varel couldn't hide his fear when he responded.

"Agree to fight me as men do or you can die without honor." Coal really sounded furious over that last prospect. "I know you want my woman and may come after her again. I won't allow that to happen. One way or another, this ends here and now."

Varel took his time in deciding. "No weapons, just you and me." He paused. "How do I know you won't shoot me if I walk in there?"

"I want to kill you with my bare hands." The rage audible in Coal's voice left no doubt that he meant every word he said.

"Fine. I'm coming and I'm unarmed."

"Don't trust him," Jill called out softly.

Coal's shot her a glare over his shoulder. "I told you to leave."

"I love you. Pay attention to them instead of me." She jerked her head toward the open door. "Here he comes." *Please win*, she silently added.

Varel stepped into the cargo hold with his arms up, palms showing, and looked furious. Coal stepped out from behind the crates gripping his weapon. Varel's eyes widened before he paled.

"I shouldn't have trusted a metal head."

Coal calmly threw his weapon aside to land somewhere near the bulkhead, far from the captain. "I have honor. You kidnapped my woman and you attempted to force her to have sex with you." He moved back to the center of the room slowly, never taking his eyes off his adversary. "I'm going to make you hurt for that." Coal's fingers waved him forward as he took a defensive stance. "Fight as if you know what it truly is to be a male."

"Shit," Sky muttered. "My friend Coal there is going to take you apart, slime ball." He paused. "I have your back, Coal. If any of his crew moves, I'll take them out. You just worry about him. I have their locations locked, though they are staying out of visual range. I'll know if they try to sneak up on us. It's probably their plan to do that with the distraction of the fight."

"I'm aware. It would be mine." Coal waved the captain closer. "Let this begin. I'm eager to see you bleed."

Varel had to step over the dead man on the deck, his boots leaving a trail of blood. He advanced slowly, taking in every inch of Coal's six-and-a-half-foot frame.

"I could make you rich, cyborg. She's just a woman. I could show you a hundred of them for you to choose from if you allow me to have her. Jillian's not even beautiful and her legs are too short. Wouldn't you enjoy a thinner woman who stands at least six feet tall? She's even a bit pudgy."

Another growl emanated from Coal. "You insult my woman and my loyalty to her as well?"

"Stupid," Sky snorted.

Varel frowned. "Name what you want."

"For you to die," Coal stated. He took an aggressive step forward. "Fight or don't but I'm about to hit you."

Varel threw a punch first, as soon as they were close enough to attack each other. Coal allowed it to land on his chest. A cold grin flashed.

"Is that the best you have?"

He threw one himself, sending Varel stumbling back but the man remained on his feet. Varel backed up and his hand suddenly went behind him, whipping out a knife with a long, wicked blade.

"I'm going to slice you up, you oversized lab reject."

Coal snarled, advancing again on the captain. Jill wanted to yell for Coal to be careful but she feared he'd look away from that nasty-looking blade that slashed out at his gut a second later.

Coal's body bowed to avoid the deadly weapon and his fist slammed hard into Varel's face. Blood bloomed where his nose took the hit but the captain slashed again, seeming not to feel the pain. Jill watched the ghastly dance as Varel lunged again to cut Coal but the bigger cyborg had great reflexes, dodging it again.

Movement by the door drew Jill's gaze as three of the crew rushed forward. Sky stepped from behind the crate, firing at them. He hit two of the crew but a third one hit the deck in a roll, crashing into crates. A fourth crew member rushed out next. Sky fired but the man behind the crate fired at him. Sky crouched, fired, and then fired again. He hit the new man who went down but the one hiding behind the crate exchanged more fire with him.

Coal and Varel seemed oblivious to the battle. Sky kept exchanging fire with the surviving crew member of the *Cutter* to keep him pinned down. Jill turned her head, wondering if she would be able to crawl the length of the pod to sneak up on the man behind the crates. He happened to be on her side of the shuttle. She went to her hands and knees and started to move forward but a hand gripped her ankle.

Jill turned her head to peer at Rune. The android shook her head and then dropped to her hands and knees, crawling forward until they were shoulder to shoulder.

"It is too dangerous."

Jill knew that. "He could shoot Coal if Sky doesn't keep him pinned down."

"I will go."

"You're programmed not to harm humans. You said so yourself."

"My programming doesn't prevent me from disarming them or pushing them from behind where they hide to avoid being killed."

Jill smiled. "You're really smart."

"I have advanced programming and can adapt."

"You're awesome. Go ahead but don't get shot."

"Logically, I pose no threat to the man." She started to inch forward.

Jill lifted her head to peer around the nose of the pod. Coal and Varel still fought. She'd never suspected the captain could hold his own with a much stronger cyborg but he remained on his feet, bleeding, and it suddenly dawned on her that Coal toyed with the man. He hit him but not hard enough to drop him or shatter bones.

"Coal," she whispered, not willing to risk saying it loud enough for Coal to hear in case it distracted him. "Just kill the son of a bitch."

The next punch Coal landed snapped Varel's head back hard and Jill swore she heard a sickening, crunching sound. As she stared she saw the man's jaw hung open, blood poured out, and then Coal hit him again. The captain dropped to his knees, shock widening his eyes, and the knife dropped when both of his hands fell to his sides. Coal snarled.

"Never take someone I love from me."

Large gray hands gripped Varel's face and for an instant pure terror transformed the captain's features, knowing what would come. Coal twisted hard, snapping his neck, and then threw the limp body to the deck. He snarled again.

"Die!" A male voice yelled.

Jill gasped as the crew member suddenly stood up with his weapon aimed directly at Coal. Sky fired but the man moved, the shot missing him by inches, and Jill inwardly screamed, terrified she was about to watch the man she loved with all her heart die in front of her.

Rune suddenly stood up, grabbed the weapon, and just tore it from the shocked man's fingers. She smiled at him.

"Weapons are dangerous. I'm confiscating this to prevent you from doing harm." She backed up, holding it in her hands. Her head turned to look directly at Sky. "I am out of the line of fire at this distance."

No one moved. The crew member stood frozen, his fingers still poised as if he held the weapon, and then his angry gaze turned to Sky. "I'm unarmed. You can't shoot me."

"That is a lie," Rune cheerfully stated. "He's got two weapons tucked behind his back in the waist of his pants."

"Drop them," Sky ordered coldly.

The man hesitated. "Are you going to allow me to go if I do?"

Sky hesitated. "Drop your weapons. I won't negotiate with you."

The man clenched his jaw. "Then fuck you." He lunged for his weapon.

The sound of Sky's weapon firing made Jill finch. The blast the crew member took to the chest slammed his body hard into the bulkhead behind him. He fell down where Jill couldn't see him.

"His life functions have ceased." Rune turned, strolling out from behind the back of the second pod. "Where do you want me to put the weapon?"

Sky walked over to her and held out his hand. "I'll take it."

Rune gave it to him instantly. Her smile remained in place. "Would you like me to clean up this mess?" Her hands lowered to the hem of her dress.

"No!" Jill struggled to her feet. "No, Rune."

Sky frowned, looking at Jill. "What is going on?"

"Don't ask. Just tell her no." Jill turned then, her gaze meeting Coal's.

He didn't come toward her but remained instead next to Varel's body. Her gaze scanned Coal to make certain he wasn't injured. He had blood on both hands, his knuckles were a little torn, but she was pretty sure most of the blood wasn't his. She met his gaze again.

"I wish you'd returned to the *Jenny* as I ordered you to do." Sadness touched his expression, dulling his eyes. "I never wanted you to see the brutality I am capable of. Please don't be afraid of me, Jill."

Jill didn't hesitate to rush at him, running. She saw surprise widen his eyes as she threw her body against his, her arms wrapping tightly around his waist, her face buried in his chest, inhaling his wonderful masculine scent mixed with the irony smell of blood.

"I love you."

His arms hesitantly wrapped around her but he avoided touching her with his bloodied hands. His chin lowered to the top of her head, resting there as he hugged her back.

"I love you too, Jill. You know I'd never harm you."

Hot tears burned behind her closed eyelids. "I know that. You came for me. Thank you, Coal. I was terrified I'd never see you again."

"I will always come for you. You are everything to me."

She sniffed and pulled her face back. Coal's gaze met hers as she stared up at him, blinking back tears. "You're everything to me too. Let's get out of here. I want to go home."

Coal's body tensed in her arms and she saw a pained look in his eyes. "You wish to return to Earth?"

She shook her head. "Home is anywhere you are, Coal. I meant home to your planet. Didn't you say something about wanting to start a farm? I've learned that I'm rich. My father left me a lot of money and that's why that jerk kidnapped me. I know what bank he put all of it into and how to access it. We'll have plenty of it to start our new life together."

Coal stared down at her. "You won't need money on Garden."

"Then, it will always be there if we do need it in the future. You're all I need, Coal."

* * * * *

Jill didn't look at him with fear or disgust. Coal had worried that she would see him differently after he killed Varel in front of her. He'd actually hesitated for a while in ending the man's life not, wishing her to see his brutal side—his cyborg side. His rage had taken over eventually. The man had taken Jill away and for that he had to die.

She still loves me, he thought, smiling down at her upturned face. It was the most beautiful thing he'd ever seen when she looked at him that way.

"We're going home."

He didn't mention that he might end up locked in a cell for the crimes he'd committed to reach her. It didn't matter. They wouldn't kill him and would consider his special circumstances when they decided his punishment. Jill would be considered his property on Garden since law stated humans belonged to cyborgs. They couldn't take her from him. That's all that mattered.

"What about her?" Sky drew his attention, his head tipping toward Rune.

The android female smiled at him when Coal studied her. She'd saved Jill from being raped and she'd also saved his life by disarming a human holding a weapon on him. He hesitated, uncertain of what to do.

"She is coming with us," Jill answered.

Coal smiled at her, feeling warmth spread through his chest. "You really do collect strays." He loved her soft heartedness.

"I do."

"She really isn't a sex bot?" Disbelief laced Sky's voice. "She looks like one to me, considering the way they built her."

"They created me to be one." Rune crossed her arms over her chest.

242

"Hot damn," Sky grinned.

"I advise you not to think like that." Jill chuckled. "They gave her advanced android technology that allows her to adapt and think for herself. She's decided she really doesn't want anyone to touch her. If you try, she's going to lock you in a cabinet until you change your mind about wanting her that way."

Sky's mouth dropped open, his strangely attractive eyes narrowing. "Seriously?"

"Jill is not lying." Rune smiled. "Keep your fluids away from me."

Coal laughed, amused at Sky's astonished expression. He hugged Jill and then slowly released her. "Come on. Let's go home." His smile died. "We'll talk about a serious matter after we use the foam-cleanser unit."

He hated to see worry on Jill's delicate features. "Is everything all right? Please tell me now. I've had enough to worry over lately."

"I'm sure it won't be too bad. I believe I am in some trouble. I had to steal the *Jenny* to come after you and had Arm help me."

Jill frowned, her thoughts a mystery to him as she peered up at him, obviously thinking hard about something.

"You can't steal what is mine. The *Jenny* and Arm belong to me and as my husband-to-be, they belong to you too as far as I'm concerned."

"Good defense," Sky mumbled. "Logical. I'd go with that one if they pull you in front of the council. Your woman also offered to help us save Councilman Zorus without asking for anything in return. With your history and what our women have done to you, hell, you may just get away with this stunt you pulled."

243

He really hoped that would be the case as he forced a smile to reassure Jill. "I am certain they will at least be lenient on me."

"If not, we have the *Jenny*." Jill's chin rose and determination shone in her eyes. "All that matters is we're together. I don't need a farm, Coal. I just need you."

Coal relaxed. "You'd live in space with me to avoid my being punished?"

"In a heartbeat. We're in love and that means everything."

Love filled him until it actually hurt. He finally knew pure happiness for the first time in his life. "It means everything to me as well," he rasped, overcome with emotion. "You are my life."

Chapter Fifteen

Two weeks later

"Arm! You're tracking in mud, darn it." Jill frowned at the android. "Remember what I said about getting it off before you come aboard?"

Two arms wrapped around her waist and pulled her back into a bare, hot chest. She grinned, all her irritation fleeing. She turned her head, lifted her chin, and grinned up at Coal.

"I'll clean the deck." He winked. "I'll also work more on his programming until he learns to check before he enters the cargo hold."

"Thanks." Her fingers curled around his at her waist. "Are you and Fray done cutting through the bulkheads?"

He chuckled. "Yes. It seems I enjoy demolition work. Our space is much bigger after we combined the two rooms. Roid has finished transferring his charging station now that he's rooming with Arm. I'm glad they don't care if they have to double up."

"I didn't want Arm and Rune sharing a room. He learned some pretty offensive jokes about blonde women from the military. I don't want to wake up some morning to find she's tried to reprogram him the way she did the onboard computer."

Coal laughed. "She's just trying to be helpful. I have to admit that I'm partial to some of the upgrades she installed. I can't remote link with my damaged implants but now everything is voice activated. It's very convenient."

"True." She let go of his hands and turned in his embrace. She wrapped her arms around his neck as she went up on tiptoe. "But did you knock out the coms in our room? I really don't want Arm rushing in again because the computer tells him I'm being attacked."

Coal's palms rubbed her ass, massaging her, and a chuckle escaped his parted lips. "It's not their fault they can't tell the difference between a fight and sex."

"That wasn't funny!"

He had the nerve to laugh again, deeper this time. "You have to admit the humor found in the situation. I will never forget you trying to explain to him that having my cock buried inside you from behind wasn't harming you and that all the sounds we made were just things we do together when we're happy." He lifted her higher up his body until she wrapped her legs around his waist. "I'm feeling the need for some real joy right now. Are you?"

"Yes." She grinned back at him. "Take me to our room." She gripped him tighter, the vee of her pants grinding against the hard erection trapped in his pants. "You feel like a lot of fun right now."

He turned with her in his arms. "The wall is right there. Arm knows now I'm not attacking you."

"Rune is outside. You never know with her how she will react about sex and she may come inside. I don't want to ever see her shove you on your ass again, thinking she's protecting me. I love your coloring but dark bruises aren't so hot to stare at there."

"You stare at my ass?"

"All the time. It's one of my favorite things to do."

"What else do you wish to see?"

"You stepping out of those pants and boots."

"We'll order her to stay outside for a while."

"Okay. Our room seems too far away right now." She tilted her head and pressed her face against the side of his neck. She kissed him there, teasing him with her tongue.

Coal groaned. "I love when you do that."

"Get out of those pants and I'll kiss a more interesting place. You love that too."

He walked quickly to the open exterior door of the shuttle. "I believed my punishment of having to live in the shuttle instead of them building us a house on the parcel of land they gave us would be difficult but I don't mind at all." He suddenly halted, studying her face closely. "I am sorry you are being punished as well. You have to live here with me."

Jill smiled, moving to his earlobe. Her teeth raked the sensitive skin there. "Anywhere we are is home and the view is a lot better on Garden than if we were living on the *Jenny* in space. As punishments go, this one is pretty easy."

He didn't look convinced. "An actual house would be more comfortable for you, Jill. This isn't what I planned when I told you we'd be happy on Garden."

She hesitated. "They had to ground the *Jenny* anyway to keep her from ever leaving the surface and I'm grateful they let me keep her. I've grown attached. I still want to keep it here once we obtain permission to have a

247

house built when your probation is over. The androids can keep living here to give us some privacy in our new home. I was more afraid they'd lock you up or separate us."

"If I had been imprisoned for attacking my fellow cyborg brothers it wouldn't have been for long since I didn't harm them. They couldn't take you from me, Jill. Unfortunately, you are still considered my property but hopefully one day that law will change." He gave her a small smile. "You own my heart and soul."

"That's why I don't mind this whole 'people being possessions' in our case." She chuckled. "We know we belong together so the paperwork doesn't matter."

"You still shouldn't be punished for what I did."

"That guy we rescued from Earth scared me the most since everyone seemed to think he was such a dick but he wanted to give you a break."

Coal shrugged his shoulders. "Zorus and I have things in common and he understood how much you mean to me." He paused. "I think he feels alone, though he is surrounded by our people. I felt that way, as if I didn't fit when I finally had my freedom, but you make me whole."

Tears flooded her eyes. "Me too. That's how you make me feel." She cleared her choked-up voice. "We need to have some fun." She winked. "And be happy they thought us living on a shuttle together would be a bad thing."

"Let me just order Rune to do something that will occupy her time." He walked to the door, still carrying Jill wrapped around him.

"Sounds good." She licked her lips and went for his ear, knowing how sensitive he would be there and how hard it would make him. She nipped the lower edge of it and his hold on her tightened.

"No." Coal halted again.

She released his ear, pulling back. "I thought you liked that. Did I bite you too hard?"

He met her gaze. "I love it when you use your teeth on me. That isn't the problem." He cleared his throat. "Rune decided to water the seeds she planted."

"So?"

Coal blinked and then cocked his head a little to peer over her shoulder. "She's using a lot of water."

"Oh no." Jill turned her head and then groaned.

Rune had removed her dress and stood with a hose spraying water over the garden she'd started. The android had a real interest in the idea of how a seed could grow into vegetation. She'd taken it as her personal mission to create a thriving food source for Coal and Jill. The naked android turned, spotted them, and waved.

Coal released Jill's ass to wave back. "Should I order her inside?" Coal turned his head and visibly winced. "The males from the next plot over are watching her."

Jill followed his gaze. At least twenty cyborg males stood at the fence watching Rune with utter fascination. They obviously preferred to watch Rune than work on their construction jobs, building the large greenhouse that would help supply the city with fresh vegetables.

"I'll go out there to explain again why she needs to remain covered."

Jill turned her head, watching Coal frowning at Rune. She'd worried he might see the android's body and find hers lacking in comparison. She couldn't compete with manufactured perfection but he'd never shown interest in Rune as a sexual object. He seemed oblivious to all that perfect synthetic skin. She slowly smiled, knowing without a doubt how deeply he loved her. She was the only woman he wanted.

"She's safe, right?"

"Yes."

She glanced at the gawking cyborgs. "Leave her there. She seems busy, that's a lot of ground to water, and it should occupy her for a while." She grinned at Coal. "There's a wall I want you to pin me against."

"What about the males? They won't venture onto our space or attempt to approach her but we should make her dress."

"Let them watch her. She really has a thing about not soiling her clothes, will just argue with us the way she usually does if we try to change something about her way of thinking, and I want to take advantage of her being occupied. A lot of cyborgs seem to think there's nothing redeeming on Earth but maybe she'll make some of them change their minds." Jill suddenly laughed. "Rune can be the good will ambassador from Earth."

Coal smiled. "Good will?"

"She looks really good and I bet every guy out there will remember there's something they still like about humans since she resembles one."

"Jill…" Coal chuckled, turning. "You know that's naughty but then, I love that about you."

"I'm in that kind of mood."

"How naughty do you feel?"

She ran her tongue over her lips, watching passion build in Coal's handsome face. "Put me down."

He lowered her instantly and Jill reached for the front of his pants, unfastening them, until his heavy, thick cock was free. She dropped to her knees, her eyes lifting to meet his.

"You do enjoy me kissing you."

"Take off your pants."

She hesitated and then rose, happy she hadn't put on shoes yet. She wiggled out of them and then removed the shirt. *Rune isn't the only one who likes to walk around without clothes on sometimes.* She grinned at the thought.

Coal grabbed her before she could go to her knees again. She gasped when he used his strength to bend her over his forearm, turning her easily, and gripped her thigh with his free hand. He gently eased them to the floor until he curved around her back, caging her in his arms on her hands and knees.

"I thought we were going to do some kissing. It's tough to do that with me facing away from you."

"Spread your thighs wide apart."

She hesitated but when he spread his, giving her room, she did the same. His chest rose from her back and she watched him reposition until his legs slid between her thighs and he sat on the deck, her ass against his chest. She turned her head to frown at him.

"What are we doing? I thought you were going to take me from behind."

"This is a position I read about on the computer. It's called 'sixty-nine position lying down'."

As he spoke, he lay back flat, his hands gripping her hips, and lifted her, pulling her back until her pussy hovered over his mouth. Jill turned her focus on his lap, right under her face. His cock lay against his belly, stiff and firm, the crown of it touching her chin.

Jill couldn't help but laugh. Coal read fiction files with sex in them sometimes, stating that he didn't want her to grow bored with him, and would surprise her with new positions every few days. She'd told him she could never tire of him touching her but she didn't complain when he read something new and promptly shared it with her.

"Am I too heavy on top of you?"

"No." He adjusted his arm, wrapping it around her hips at his chest to lock her body there. His face nuzzled between her thighs. "Spread wider for me and move a little closer to my mouth."

She had to wiggle a little but the top of her thighs ended up braced against the top of Coal's broad shoulders. She moaned when he lifted his head, his free hand spreading her pussy lips open to allow his mouth to fasten over her clit.

"Oh God."

He removed his mouth. "Kiss me back." His mouth returned to her clit, sealing around the swelling bud, and his hot tongue rubbed the very sensitive nerve endings there.

Jill parted her lips, easily capturing the hard flesh pressing against her, and took inches of his cock into her welcoming mouth. Coal instantly responded by groaning against her clit, creating wonderful vibrations. She sucked on him slowly at first but then faster, taking more of him deeper inside.

The sweet taste of him nearly drove her insane when the pleasure threatened to overcome her. The faster she rode his cock with her mouth, he responded in turn on her clit. When one of his fingers breached her pussy, rubbing against her clenching vaginal walls, she knew she would not last long. Her climax hovered as the need to come became painfully intense.

Coal's hips started to squirm, his moans grew louder, and the vibrations on her clit increased. A strong jerk of his cock against her tongue told her he had reached the point that he couldn't hold back any longer. He cried out, sucking her swollen bud frantically with hard tugs, and his release filled her mouth. Jill swallowed every drop, loving his sweet flavor, and trying to hold off her own rapturous explosion when his finger left her. She guessed he'd need a few seconds to recover but instead two of his fingers suddenly drove into her. The sensation of being stretched and filled while he pushed in deep, combined with his incredible kisses, rocketed her over the edge. She managed to jerk her mouth away from his cock just before she screamed out his name, coming so hard she nearly passed out.

Time lost all meaning for Jill while she lay sprawled over the man she loved. Her cheek rested on his thigh, his cock mere inches from her lips, and she grinned, watching his sensitive testicles respond to the warm air she breathed over them. Coal eased his fingers out of her, his tongue

253

swiping her clit slowly for one last lick, making her shiver from another mild aftershock of her climax. Coal chuckled, rested his head back against the floor, and turned his face to nuzzle her inner thigh.

"I liked that one."

"I learned another one. It involves tying you down."

Jill pushed up from his thigh and lifted her head to grin at him over her shoulder. Interest sparked her libido again. "I'm listening."

"We need to change positions."

She hated to get up but she wanted him more. She rolled off him to sprawl on her back. The cool metal of the deck soothed her heated flesh. Coal sat up while he slowly took in every inch of her naked skin until his gaze met hers. Passion still darkened his eyes.

"Would you trust me tie you down? I know how vulnerable you would feel."

She saw a flash of pain in his eyes, obviously sparked from a memory from his past. Jill sat up quickly and straddled his lap. Sitting there nearly made their faces level. She wrapped her arms tightly around his neck and her breasts pushed against his muscular, hard chest. She couldn't miss how his cock hardened, trapped between their bellies.

"I love you, I trust you, and you can tie me up any time you want to."

His features softened. "One day I want you to tie me down."

She tried to hide her surprised reaction but Coal could obviously read her too well.

254

"I love and trust you too, Jill. I need to replace those memories of the bad things done to me while being restrained with good ones of you doing wonderful things to me that I want to happen between us. You deserve a male who faces his fears to get beyond them."

"I understand but I don't think anything is wrong with you. I hate that you were hurt, I want to kill every damn one of those women who forced you to breed them, but what breaks my heart the most is that you can't see how courageous you are to have survived it all."

"I'm damaged." His jaw clenched.

"No, Coal." She smiled at him. "To me, you're perfect just the way you are. I love everything about you."

* * * * *

Coal stared deeply into Jill's beautiful eyes. She didn't attempt to hide how sincerely she meant her words. She thought he didn't need to be fixed, that he was the male she wanted, and she didn't see his flaws.

Her face blurred and he knew his own tears filled his eyes. He blinked rapidly but they wouldn't be hidden from the woman who had changed his life. She didn't look horrified as he shed them. She leaned forward to kiss each one that slid down his cheeks instead.

This is happiness, he thought. *Love. Acceptance. Jill gives me all of this and so much more.* Then another thought struck him that made him chuckle.

"What's funny?" Jill grinned at him. "Share."

"I realized the past doesn't matter. My future with you will be filled with a lot of fun." He winked. "And love."

"So much of that," Jill nodded, and brushed a kiss over his mouth.

He ached to make love to her again. "You heal me, Jill. You make all the pain I've suffered fade away with every day we are together—with each touch, word, and look."

"You do the same for me."

Her hand reached between them. He softly groaned against her mouth when her fingers brushed the shaft of his cock, teasing the underside of it with her featherlight touches.

"Yes," he rasped, his hands sliding down her back to cup her ass, pulling her tighter against his aching cock, longing to be sheathed inside her hot, tight pussy that sent him to heaven. "Love is a wonderful thing."

"And hot sex," she moaned.

Coal couldn't agree more.

19561121R00153

Printed in Poland
by Amazon Fulfillment
Poland Sp. z o.o., Wrocław